Bottletops For Battleships
Sylvie's War

Also by Andrea Gilbey

Three Finger Exercises
Short Story Collection

Bottletops For Battleships
Sylvie's War

Edelweiss For Elizabeth
Sylvie's Peace

Yours Ever, Notch

Anthologies

XX: SIW Goes Platinum
The Indian Creek Anthology Series, Vol. 20

Herding Cats and Other Alien Creatures
The Indian Creek Anthology Series, Vol. 21

Apollo and Athena Walk Into A Bar: Art Meets Science
The Indian Creek Anthology Series, Vol. 22

Children's Books

A Horse, Of Course!

A Horse, Of Course!
Coloring book

A Horse, Of Course!
Activity book

You're a Big Sister!

You're a Big Brother!

Bottletops For Battleships
Sylvie's War

Andrea Gilbey

Per Bastet

Bottletops For Battleships: Sylvie's War

Second Edition

Copyright © 2020 Andrea Gilbey

ALL RIGHTS RESERVED

No part of this book may be reproduced or transmitted in any form or by any means, electronic or mechanical, including photocopying, recording, or by any information storage or retrieval system, without prior written permission from the copyright owner unless such copying is expressly permitted by federal copyright law. The publisher is not authorized to grant permission for further uses of copyrighted selections printed in this book. Permission must be obtained from the individual copyright owners identified herein. Requests for permission should be addressed to the publisher.

Published by Per Bastet Publications LLC, P.O. Box 3023 Corydon, IN 47112

Cover art by Andrea Gilbey

ISBN 978-1-942166-70-2

This is a work of fiction. Names, characters, places and incidents are products of the author's imagination or are used for literary purpose and are not to be construed as real. Any resemblance to actual events, locales, organizations, or persons, living or dead, are entirely coincidental. The names of actual locations and products are used solely for literary effect and should neither be taken as endorsement nor as a challenge to any associated trademarks.

First Edition: 2015

Available in trade paperback and DRM-free ebook formats

Dedicated To:

Sheila and Bert Gilbey
Alice and Harry Wells
Doris and Harry Gilbey

With Grateful Thanks To:

Marian Allen
Ginny Fleming
Brian Gilbey
Colleen Gruver
Jerri Keele
Angela Painter
Jenny Painter
Sjaniek Schaap

Bottletops For Battleships
Sylvie's War

Part One
1939

Andrea Gilbey

Chapter One

"This Country Is At War With Germany"

I knew something was up when Mum sat down in the front room in her apron. On a Sunday, and all!

"Tom, it's five to eleven," she said.

Daddy slowly folded up his newspaper, rested his pipe on the glass ashtray, and reached up to the wireless on the mantelpiece. "Click" went the knob as he turned it, and the sound slowly floated into the room. Tiny specks of dust danced in the sunlight streaming through the window.

Oh, the news. Boring.

My parents had been doing a lot of serious talking about the news lately, after I was in bed, and sometimes I would creep onto the stairs and sit quietly and listen, but I didn't really understand what they were saying; something about a war, but I knew the war had happened years ago, before I was born, before even some of my aunts and uncles were born. I knew that Uncle Robert and Uncle William had died in the war, and that Mum and Daddy went to the war memorial in the village once a year to remember their brothers.

"Mum, this year, can I. . . ," I started.

"Shhh . . . Sylvie," interrupted Mum, "this is important, be quiet for a few minutes, there's a good girl." She held my hand and gave it a quick squeeze.

The newsreader was speaking very seriously. It was the man with the nice calm voice, Al Varly-Dell. Maureen-next-door said it wasn't spelt like that, his name was Alvar Lidell, but what kind of a name was Alvar?

Anyway, however-you-spell-him was introducing the Prime Minister, Mr Chamberlain. I sat up very straight. I know people on the wireless can't see you, but it's respectful, isn't it, like standing up for God Save The King at the pictures.

Mr Chamberlain spoke slowly and his voice sounded sad and sorry, as though he didn't want to say what he was about to tell us.

"This morning, the British Ambassador in Berlin handed the German Government a final note stating that, unless we heard from them by eleven o'clock that they were prepared at once to withdraw their troops from Poland, a state of war would exist between us.

"I have to tell you now that no such undertaking has been received, and that, consequently, this country is at war with Germany."

Mum was still holding my hand, and her grip had got tighter and tighter. I wriggled my fingers a bit, to try to tell her to loosen her hold. She took in a very deep breath, looked down at me and smiled. Her eyes looked very shiny bright, and her smile was a bit lopsided. She hugged me tight and kissed the top of my head.

"We'll be all right, dear, don't you worry."

Should I worry? I'd never really worried about anything on the news before, it was grown-ups' stuff.

Mum gave me another squeeze and slowly got up off the settee.

"Those spuds won't roast themselves; I'd better get on."

She walked briskly back into the kitchen, her slippers scuffling on the lino, and I heard her blow her nose. I could hear Audrey snuffling in her cot upstairs and cocked an ear; if she started crying it was my job to run up and play with her until she settled again.

Mr Chamberlain was still talking away on the wireless, explaining how he and the other men in the Government had tried to stop a war happening, but Daddy reached up and turned the switch to off.

"It doesn't matter what they tried now, does it, Ducky, we're at war again."

"Will you have to go and fight, Daddy, Like Uncle Robert and Uncle William did? I don't want you to go. . . ." I started to cry.

Daddy cuddled up beside me and wrapped his arm around me.

"No, Ducks, I won't have to go, I'm too old, for one thing; I'm over forty now, they won't want an old feller like me getting in the way, and they'll want all the older men who work on the farms and nurseries to stay and help grow food. You heard what Mr Chamberlain said, they're going to start up a Home Guard for the older men and the boys who are too young to fight; between all of us we'll keep you, Audrey, and Mummy safe, don't worry."

"And what about school? Will there still be school?" This was an important point; I would be five years old next month and I was due to start school tomorrow!

"Yes, school will start up again as usual, we're not going to let a load of silly Germans with their silly walk stop us going about our business, are we!"

Daddy jumped up and started goose-stepping around the room, talking in a gibberish language that sounded like the film reel we'd seen at the pictures of that Her Hitler. I still didn't understand why a man wanted to be called "Her".

Mum came and stood in the kitchen doorway, shaking her head.

"Tom, don't be so disrespectful, this is serious," she said, but she couldn't help laughing.

"It's a lovely sunny day, dinner's in the oven, and we're all together and safe. Let's enjoy it while we can, eh Ducks?" said Daddy, chucking Mum under the chin.

"Come on, Sylvie, let's go down the garden and pick some peas to have with that lamb, but you have to whistle while you pop them, remember?"

Daddy always said that when we popped peas; if we were whistling we couldn't eat the fresh, juicy peas as they came out of the pods.

I ran ahead down the garden to the vegetable patch, past the Anderson shelter that Daddy had dug into the ground a few months ago. I liked playing in the shelter when it was dry, but if it had been raining the floor was very wet in there, and if it was a hot day the metal sides heated up so that going in there was like walking into the glasshouses on the nursery where Daddy worked.

We picked enough pea pods for dinner and popped them into the colander to take indoors, whistling "Lily of Laguna" all the time. As we turned to go back into the house an awful noise started up, a long up and down wailing noise. Daddy grabbed my hand, "Come on, into the shelter . . . I didn't expect it to come this soon. . . ."

"What about Mummy and Audrey?" I cried, trying to pull him to the house.

"Mummy knows what to do," he reassured me, and sure enough, there was Mum coming out of the back door with Audrey in her arms. We climbed down into the shelter and sat silently, listening, apart from Audrey, who was babbling with excitement at being woken from her nap. Scamp settled down on the floor between us, thinking it was a new game.

"I can't hear any planes." said Mum.

"No," replied Daddy, "it's too quiet for it to be a real raid, maybe it's a practice."

He turned to me. "Sylvie, when you hear that up and down siren, wherever you are, you must get into a shelter immediately, do you understand? At school they will tell you what to do, and you know where the shelter is in the park if the siren goes while you're walking home, don't you?"

I nodded solemnly. Now I understood what the shelter was *for*, but what were we sheltering *from*? I decided not to ask; it was all very confusing and worrying, I would deal with this war thing in small pieces, a bit at a time.

Suddenly the noise started up again, but this time the tone got higher and higher, then stayed on the high note, rather than going up and down.

"It must have been a test," said Daddy. "That long steady note means 'all clear' and you can come out of the shelter. Will you remember that, Sylvie?"

"Yes, Daddy," I answered. "The up and *down* noise means you have to go *down* into the shelter, and the noise that *goes up* and stays up means you can *come up* and stay up!"

Mummy and Daddy looked at each other and laughed, then Mum suddenly exclaimed, "Oh! The potatoes!" and ran indoors.

We followed her in and found Audrey sitting awkwardly in her high chair where Mum had plonked her down, laughing and banging her spoon on the table, as Mum took a smoking tray of blackened potatoes from the oven.

"The first casualty of the war," joked Mum, "my roast spuds! Blast that Hitler!"

But Daddy and I looked at each other and smiled. We loved crispy, overcooked roast potatoes!

Chapter Two

Good Morning

The sun gets up quite early in September, but I got up even earlier on my first day of school.

I ran downstairs to the bathroom to have a wash and heard the creak of the kitchen door as Daddy collected his bicycle from the lean-to. Daddy hadn't left for work yet, I was so early!

He heard me padding across the kitchen and turned with a smile, "Good luck at school, Ducky, be good!" He kissed me, bent to fasten his bicycle clips, and wheeled his bike down the garden, whistling.

I washed quickly but properly; I knew Mum would send me back to do it again if she thought I'd skimped; and ran back upstairs to dress in the clothes that were hanging on the wardrobe door: my blue pleated skirt with its attached bodice that buttoned at the shoulders, and my striped short-sleeved jumper that Mum knitted for me.

Audrey stood at the bottom of her cot, holding on to the top rail and jumping up and down saying, "Silly go cool!" which was her way of saying "Sylvie's going to school." I didn't much like her calling me Silly, but I hoped she'd grow out of it. She was only eighteen months old.

As I finished dressing, Mum came into the room and handed me a clean hankie, which I tucked into the pocket of my knickers, just above my knee.

I was too excited to want much breakfast, but I forced down a slice of buttered toast and a cup of milky tea, then it was time to leave for school. I picked up my satchel; the same tan leather satchel that Mummy had used at school.

Mum came with me that first day, but I knew the way to school, it wasn't far, with only our road to cross, and no-one in our road owned a car, so there was no traffic.

We crossed the road, walked round the corner, along the footpath at the side of the park, and came to the school playground. All the children were running and playing in the sunshine, and for just a minute I felt a bit scared, it was so busy, then I saw lots of children I knew; there was Maureen-next-door, the twins, Brenda and Beryl from across the road, and Georgie Bird from next door but one. We always called Georgie "Dickie" Bird, but not when his dad could hear us!

A tall lady came out of the long, low school building and rang a hand bell. That must be Miss Manning, the headmistress. All the children who had been at school the year before knew what to do and lined up in chattering groups, boys on the left, girls on the right, ready to file into the school. I could already read, so I knew that the words over the two doors of the school building said "Girls" and Boys", and guessed that we had to go in through separate entrances. But why?

As the older children marched into school, another lady came out, and I knew her! It was Miss Eames. Her father worked at the nursery at High Trees with Daddy. I had seen her during the summer when Daddy took me to work with him one day, and she had come to the nursery to deliver her father's dinner.

She looked at me and smiled, then said, "All you new children, line up here in front of me. Tomorrow you will make two lines, boys that side, girls this side, as you just saw the other children do, but today we will all walk in together."

We marched into school and Miss Eames led us to our classroom.

It was a high-ceilinged room with windows set right up at the tops of the walls, too high for me to see out even if I stood on a chair.

Spaced around the rooms were tall lengths of new wood, wedged firmly between floor and ceiling. It looked like the room was full of trees, and the wood smelled really nice! I wondered what those pieces of wood were for.

We were told where to sit, and I beamed when I found out I would be sharing a double desk with Maureen-next-door. We started chatting excitedly about how different everything was, then Miss Eames called us to attention by clapping her hands.

"Class One, I am going to call the register now. When I say your name, you must reply 'present!' so I know you are here. Are we ready?"

We all replied "Yes, Miss!" and Miss Eames started calling out one name after another.

When she called my proper name, "Sylvia Ford", Maureen giggled and I nudged her as I replied, "Present!"

That first morning we didn't do any proper lessons, we were given our writing books and pencils, and told to write our names on the books, and then Miss Eames called us up to her desk one by one to hear us say the alphabet, read, if we could, and do some counting, while the rest of the class drew pictures of their family, pets, friends, or whatever we wanted to draw. I found it all easy and fun to do.

At eleven o'clock by the classroom clock we were told to line up by the door and file into the hall. As we marched into the big room, Miss Manning was standing at the door, and as the children passed her they muttered what sounded like, "Miss Manning, Miss Manning," which I thought was a bit odd, but I muttered it just like everyone else.

Miss Manning explained that Assembly, which was apparently what this was called when the whole school was in the same room, would be first thing in the morning, starting from tomorrow, and that the first thing we did every day after we said our prayers together would be "handkerchief drill". Miss Manning would say "Has everyone remembered their clean handkerchief?" and we were all to take our hankies out and wave them!

She then became serious and started talking about the war. She explained that the school was a very safe place to be, and that if we heard the air raid siren during class we were to crawl under our desks and stay still unless our teachers told us to do anything else.

We were to make sure we had our gas masks with us every day, and our class teachers would check every morning to make sure that we did.

I hated my gas mask. It was sitting in its cardboard box on my desk, squatting there, waiting for something bad to happen so I had to use it. I knew how to put it on, we had all been shown when we went to the church hall to collect them, but I hoped I never had to wear it. It had a horrible rubbery smell, and people looked frightening and not like themselves when they had their masks on. Mine was a brightly coloured child's mask; they called them "Mickey Mouse" masks, which didn't make it any better to my way of thinking, I'd seen Mickey Mouse at the pictures and didn't think much of him, he had a silly squeaky voice. I preferred Pluto.

We marched back to our classrooms and Miss Eames explained the school rules, then it was dinner time, which Miss Eames called "lunch".

We marched back to the hall again — there was a lot of marching about at school, I had discovered — which was set out with long tables. Each class sat at its own table, with a teacher at the head of the table, but not our own class teacher. This was so that all the teachers and children could get to know each other.

I recognised the teacher at our table. It was Miss Hills who lived in one of the bigger houses at the end of our road, which she shared with another of the kindergarten teachers and one of the teachers from the "Big Girls'" school. I sat at the end of the table next to her, which turned out to be a mistake, as when she dished up the food we had to pass the plates to our right, so I had to pass everyone else's dinner round under my nose before I got mine.

Dinner, sorry, lunch, was cheese and potato pie, and it had a lovely crispy layer of almost-burnt cheese on the top, which I saved until last.

Miss Hills leaned down and said quietly, "Sylvia, if you don't want the crust of your pie may I have it?"

"Oh no Miss!" I answered anxiously, "I like the crust, I'm saving it for last!"

Miss Hills laughed, "Sensible girl! So would I!"

~*~

When lunch was over we ran out to play, and I saw that some of the older children had brought skipping ropes, balls, and marbles to school to play with. Maureen and I sat on the step of the girls' entrance and watched everything, talking all the time about what we thought of school.

"I don't feel like I've learned everything yet, do you, Sylvie?" asked Maureen.

"No," I replied, "but it's only the first day."

"What, do we have to come back again tomorrow?" Maureen joked, and we fell about laughing.

Just before the bell rang for afternoon school, a man in overalls propped a ladder up against the playground fence and started painting on the school sign! When we marched back into class, Maureen and I ran up to Miss Eames.

"Miss, Miss!" we cried, "there's a man painting on the school sign! He shouldn't be doing that!"

"Don't worry, girls," said Miss Eames, "Miss Manning asked him to do it; he's changing the sign from 'Kindergarten' to 'Infants' School.'"

"Why, Miss?" I asked.

Miss Eames paused and thought for a moment as though she wasn't sure how to answer us. "I suppose because it's easier to say," she replied, vaguely. "Now go to your seats, I'm going to put a writing exercise on the board to see how neatly you can all write."

When the three o'clock bell rang, it felt like we had been in school for years, it was such a long day, and so many things to remember! Maureen and I ran home, chattering all the way, and agreed that whichever of us was ready first would call for the other in the morning so we could walk to school together. We said goodbye and I ran into the house as Mum opened the door.

"Well? Did you have a good day?" she smiled.

"Oh yes!" I gabbled, "We did drawing, and reading, and writing, and my teacher is Miss Eames, you know, her father works with Daddy, and we have to wave our hankies at Miss Manning every day, and I sit next to Maureen. . . ."

"Slow down, slow down," laughed Mum. "Save some of it for tea time, or you'll have to say it all over again when Daddy comes home!"

I ran out to play in the garden with Scamp, until Daddy came home, but I couldn't resist telling the little dog all about my day. He put his head on one side and cocked his ears as though he understood every word, then he wriggled under the fence into Maureen's garden and gambolled down to the chicken pen to bark at the hens and Mrs Fielding's big cockerel who had recently been re-named "Hitler" because of his strutting walk.

Over tea, which was bacon roly-poly for Daddy and toast and dripping for Mum and me, I finally ran out of words.

"So, you like school then?" asked Daddy.

"Yes, I do," I said, "but we do some strange things. When we go into Assembly, everyone says 'Miss Manning, Miss Manning' to the headmistress. That's a bit odd, isn't it?"

Daddy looked across the table at Mum and his mouth twitched a bit. He poured a little of his tea into his saucer to cool and sipped it slowly.

"Do you think it might be 'Good Morning, Miss Manning,' that everyone says, Ducks?"

"Oh! I think that might be it!" I exclaimed. "We don't say 'Good Morning' at home, do we, we just give each other a kiss. Let's start from tomorrow!"

"But we'll still give each other a kiss, too," said Mum.

"Oh yes, of course! But I don't think I'll kiss Miss Manning."

Part Two
1940

Chapter Three

Tomatoes, Cucumbers and Land Girls

Mum spooned the last of the carrots onto her plate and carried it over to the table. She sat down and smiled at us all as we tucked in to our fish pie. Food was rationed now because of the war, but Mum always managed to serve up a good filling tea, although I wasn't allowed to have thick butter on my bread and toast any more, I had to have margarine, thinly spread, and save the butter ration for best.

We ate in silence for a moment, then Mum cleared her throat and said, "I've got some news for all of you. I've got a job."

Daddy stopped eating, with his fork halfway to his mouth.

"Oh, Amy, there's no need for that, you do enough running the house and looking after the kids, and the Saturday morning cleaning job at the Crown brings in a bit."

I glanced between Mum and Dad. This must be serious, Daddy hardly ever called Mum "Amy" unless it was serious, it was always "Ducks" or "Dearie". I said nothing, questions were queuing up in my brain, but I wasn't sure I wanted to hear the answers.

Daddy asked one of the questions for me.

"What about the kids?"

"It's all organised, Tom, don't worry. The job is at Filers, just down the road from your Mum's, I don't start until nine, so I can see Sylvie off to school, get the bus up to High Trees and drop Audrey off at her Grandma's and walk round the corner. I finish at two, so I'll be home in time for Sylvie coming out of school. I want to do my bit for the war effort too."

"What did Mother say when you asked her to babysit?" asked Dad.

"To start with she said 'Oh Amelia' in that tone she uses when she disapproves of me," Mum winked at me and continued, "but I think she quite likes the idea. Now your John's in the navy she's only got Maude at home in the evenings, so having Audrey during the day will give her something to do."

"Other than the church flowers, cleaning at the vicarage, collecting for Alexandra Rose day and every other charity going, organising church jumble sales, and generally bossing the parish about," grinned Daddy.

"What will you do at the job, Mum?" I asked, "And what about the school holidays?" It was nearly spring half term, and I was feeling panicky about being left at home on my own.

"Don't worry about the holidays, Sylvie, you'll go to Grandma Ford's with Audrey, and maybe Mrs Brownlow next door will have her granddaughter there in the holidays. Susan, isn't it? And the job will be fun! I'm going to be growing tomatoes, cucumbers, all sorts of nice salad things, working in a glasshouse on a nursery, just like Daddy."

I carried on eating my fish pie and carrots, thinking hard.

Grandma was strict, but kind, and her house was fun. It was full of ornaments, photographs, and books. Lots of books! If Susan Brownlow was next door, I'd have someone to play with, and Audrey would be two years old in a few months and was a lot more fun to play with now she could walk and talk, although she didn't always talk sense. And at least she could say "Sylvie" now and didn't call me "Silly" in front of people.

And maybe Auntie Maude would be there on her day off.

~*~

I came downstairs on Monday morning and there was Mum, standing at the sink filling the kettle, wearing trousers! Her hair was tied up in a scarf, and Daddy's old wellingtons were standing by the back door.

We left the house together, and at the end of the road she turned in the other direction to catch the bus to High Trees. I wanted to wait until the bus came, but she waved me on my way.

"Hurry up, Sylvie, you'll be late! I'll see you later."

At playtime I asked all my friends "Does your mum work?"

Some of them said no, but a lot of people said yes, and their mothers had really interesting jobs.

Some, like Mum, worked in nurseries, growing food, some worked in shops, and one boy's mum had taken over his dad's milk round while his dad was in the army. Norma in the class above me had the mother with the most exciting job. Her mum went all the way to Woodfield, six miles away, to work in the ordnance factory, making guns and bullets.

The kitchen smelled wonderful when I opened the back door.

"Mmmmmm. . . . Tomatoes! Did you bring some home, Mum?"

"No," laughed Mum, "it's just the smell from the baby tomato plants I've been working with. When I washed my hands after work, the soap came off bright yellow from the tomato plants! The smell is still on my coat."

"Do you like the job?" I asked.

"Oh yes," she replied. "The other people who work there are really friendly. We're allowed to have a radio in the glasshouse so we can listen to Workers' Playtime, and we sing along with all the songs."

"When can I start work?!" I asked.

"What shall we do during the holiday" asked Maureen as we walked home after school broke up.

"I'm going to my Grandma's every day. I won't be able to come out to play until I get home."

Maureen scuffed along with one foot on the path and one kicking the dead leaves in the kerb.

"Oh," she said quietly.

"But we've got all weekend," I said, "and Roy Rogers is on at the Flea Pit. Maybe Daddy will take us tomorrow after he finishes work."

Maureen grabbed my hand and pumped my arm up and down.

"Oh, yes! Ask him after tea, and knock on the wall, two knocks for yes, three for no."

~*~

When we came out of the Empire Cinema — commonly known as the Flea Pit — there was a surprise waiting for us; Maureen's dad was home on leave and had come to meet us! He was still at the training camp in south London, although we weren't supposed to know that, careless talk costs lives and all that, but he had a two-day pass and had come home for the weekend. Maureen clung to her dad's arm all the way home and told him everything she'd been doing since he left, while he tried to talk to Daddy, and I "galloped" on ahead, with the hood of my coat on my head and the top button done up, the coat and sleeves flapping behind.

~*~

It was strange to get up early on a school holiday morning, but fun to catch the bus with Mum and Audrey. I liked the journey up to High Trees, because if you looked back the way you came you could see the whole of Handley spread out below, and if it was sunny the golden cockerel weather vane on the church spire winked and twinkled in the sun.

Audrey bounced on Mum's knee, as the bus was too crowded for her to sit on a seat. "Roo Roo!" she said, and laughed.

"Well, hello! Look who's here!" said Grandma, and gathered Audrey and me in a big hug. "Time for a cup of tea, Amy?"

"No thanks, Grandma, I'm a bit late, we had quite an exciting morning deciding which toys to bring," smiled Mum, ruffling my hair. "Be good, girls, I'll see you later."

"Roo Roo?" said Audrey.

"You'll see Roo Roo later, dear, now come on in."

Roo Roo?

"Helefump" said Audrey, toddling into the front room.

"Helefump?" I asked, following her in.

"It's your Uncle Johnny's old toy elephant on wheels," said Grandma. "Audrey loves him."

It was strange to see how at home Audrey was here, but of course she came to Grandma's every day, while I hadn't visited for several weeks. I wandered about the room, picking things up and putting them down again, feeling gloomy and out of place.

"Is Susan here for half term, Grandma?" I asked, flumping down into the armchair.

"No, dear, her granny said she's gone to her auntie's this time. Now, what do you want to do? Mum said you'd brought toys with you? Or do you want to help me make a carrot cake for tea? You can take a piece home for each of you."

I smiled. Hearing Grandma call Mummy "Mum" always made me chuckle a bit. I jumped up and followed Grandma to the kitchen. Mum loved carrot cake!

The cake was cooling on the worktop, and a cottage pie was in the oven, more vegetables than minced beef, but it smelled delicious. Suddenly there was a tap at the back door, the handle turned, and a cheerful rosy face, topped with a mop of brown curly hair, appeared in the doorway.

"Hello, Mrs F, I hope I'm not late?"

I watched in surprise as a grown-up girl in khaki green trousers and jumper heeled off a pair of sturdy boots on the back step and padded into the kitchen in thick socks.

She smiled at me, "You must be Audrey's big sister, Sylvie!

Your gran's told me all about you. I'm Ruby. I'm in the Land Army, working at Nailer's farm and lodging here with your gran. I've spoken to Mr Nailer and he says I can take you over there to see the pigs and horses one morning. We thought we'd keep it as a surprise for you!"

Audrey came toddling in from the front room, pushing Helefump and shouting, "Roo Roo!"

"So *that's* what Roo Roo means!" I laughed.

Chapter Four

Run, Rabbit, Run!

"Where's Ruby?" I asked excitedly, bursting into Grandma's kitchen.

"Sylvia! Where are your manners? Say good morning to Grandma properly."

"Sorry, Mummy." I stopped and looked up at them both. "Good morning, Grandma."

Grandma bent down and gave me one of her squeaky kisses, then reached out for a hug from Audrey.

"That's better," she said. "As for Ruby, she starts work at five o'clock, so she's already gone."

My face fell.

"She hasn't forgotten you, don't worry," said Grandma. "She'll come back and get you when she stops for her tea break at ten."

I looked at the clock. It was a quarter to nine. A whole hour and a quarter to wait!

"I'll see you later, girls, be good!" Mum kissed us and waved goodbye as she closed the door behind her.

"Why don't you take Audrey out into the garden and see if you can find any eggs for me?" said Grandma. "The brown hen has been looking broody, and I think she may have been laying."

She handed me a little wicker basket and opened the kitchen door. I looked anxiously at the clock. An hour and a quarter less two minutes.

"Don't worry," said Grandma again, "I'll call you in the very second Ruby gets here."

I took Audrey's hand and helped her down the back step and we started searching among the plants to see if any of Grandma's five hens had laid any eggs.

Audrey soon got bored with looking and sat down on the grass to blow dandelion clocks. "One," puff, "two," puff, "free," "puff, "four! Four o'clock, Sylvie!"

I ignored her. I was trying not to think about time.

~*~

Grandma was right, the hens had been laying. I found one brown speckled egg under the rhubarb, and another snuggled behind a patch of carnations. Only two.

I looked around the garden; the hens were busy doing what hens do, scratching and pecking and wandering about aimlessly. Then I saw the little brown hen. She was walking very deliberately and heading towards the shelter. I followed her quietly, trying not to scare her. She was going down the steps! The shelter door had been left ajar and the hen walked straight in. I peeped round the door and watched her. In the corner of the shelter was a folded blanket, nestled down into the bottom of an upturned bucket. Grandma always kept a bucket in her shelter "for emergencies".

The hen delicately stepped across the floor of the shelter and hopped up onto the bucket with a flutter of her wings. She shuffled, smoothed her feathers with her beak, and settled down.

I watched her until her eyes started to close, then slowly crept into the shelter. The chicken opened one beady eye and looked at me.

I made soft squeaky noises between my lips, the way grandma did when she approached a sitting hen, and slowly knelt down beside the bucket. I slid my hand gently under the warm soft feathers and my fingers curled around something hard and smooth. She had an egg, and she was brooding it!

I closed my hand around the egg and gently, slowly, pulled it out from under the hen. I put it in the basket and carefully climbed the steps out of the shelter. Audrey gave up her dandelion clocks and followed me into the house.

I handed the basket to Grandma and told her about the blanket nest in the shelter.

"I wonder how long she's been laying in there." said Grandma, "The last raid was over a week ago, and no-one's been down there since."

She took a large mixing bowl down from the shelf over the sink and filled it with cold water. Very carefully, she put the eggs into the water and watched them. The eggs moved slightly in the water as they rolled around, but none of them bobbed to the top of the bowl, so that meant they were all fresh and good to eat.

Grandma carefully dried the eggs and placed them in the little dimples of the egg tray, and set them in the scullery to keep cool.

I had been so engrossed in collecting the eggs I forgot to look at the time, and suddenly the back door opened and there was Ruby, in her khaki uniform.

"Hello, Sylvie." She smiled. "Are you ready for a day on the farm? I won't come in, my boots are dirty. Did you bring your sun hat?"

I ran to the front hall and grabbed my hat from the chair, kissed Grandma again, and took Ruby's hand as we walked down the garden and out through the back gate into the lane.

~*~

The field was full of long dry grass, so we walked around the edge. There was a loud chugging noise coming from the middle, and over the tops of the high grasses I could see a Land Girl, dressed just like Ruby, driving a small tractor with a big clattering machine attached to the back.

Ruby hoisted me up to sit on her shoulders so I could see what was happening.

"That's the combine harvester," she explained. "We're cutting the hay to feed the animals through the winter. You see the blades at the front going round and round? They're cutting the grass, then it goes up that belt into the baler. The baler squashes it into a rectangular block, ties it up with string, and spits it out the back."

I watched the machine for a while in silence. It was very clever, but a bit frightening at the same time. I didn't want to get too close to it.

"We use the horses for some of the machine work," said Ruby. "Because of the fuel rationing, we can only use the tractor for the hardest jobs; for things like ploughing and seeding, we use the horses."

"Can I see the horses?" I asked eagerly. I much preferred a horse to a noisy tractor!

The farmyard was busy and noisy! It was feeding time for the pigs, so Ruby took me to the barn where the pig food was stored and we filled a bucket with the woody-looking chunks of food.

I could have followed my nose to the pig sty, even if I couldn't see it. It wasn't a bad smell, it actually smelt very good and sweet, but it was strong.

Ruby rattled the bucket as we walked nearer to the sty, and the pigs came out of their shelter and trotted over to the wall. One big sow stood on her hind legs and put her front trotters on the low wall so she could watch us bring her dinner.

"Here pig, pig, pig," Ruby called. She picked up a bucket and set it upside down by the wall, but not too close, so I could stand on it and throw some food to the pigs. They snuffled and snorted among the straw to grab all the food they could find, and nudged each other out of the way with their strong snouts. Their ears were so floppy that they fell over their eyes, so they had to keep shaking their heads back to see what they were eating.

"Come on," said Ruby, lifting me down, "let's go and say hello to the horses. You have to be very careful around horses, so you must do exactly what I say, and don't make any sudden movements, all right?" I nodded and took hold of her hand again.

The horses were in their stables, some of them with their heads out over the doors watching what was going on. Another Land Girl was leading one enormous horse out of his stall and strapping a harness on him.

"Deborah's hitching Captain up to the hay rake," explained Ruby. "Once the combine's finished they'll go over the field with a big wide rake and catch up any loose hay that the baler dropped."

Captain was a beautiful dark brown horse with fluffy white feet; Ruby said he was a Shire horse.

We walked over to the stables and Ruby called softly to another horse, smaller than Captain, and a reddish brown all over.

"This horse is called Ruby!" She laughed. "It makes things a bit confusing sometimes!"

Ruby-the-horse stuck her nose out over the bottom half of her stall door and nodded her head up and down, as though she agreed. Ruby-the-girl gently stroked the horse's nose and talked to her calmly, then told me to reach up and stroke her.

The horse's nose felt like the softest velvet, and her breath was warm on my hand. I looked into her dark eyes and almost felt as though she was talking to me.

"Would you like to give her an apple, Sylvie?"

I nodded quietly, not wanting to startle the beautiful horse.

Ruby-the-girl handed me a windfall apple and showed me how to hold it out on the flat of my hand and offer it to Ruby-the-horse.

I was a bit scared as the big head swung down towards me, and I felt a blob of horse dribble land on my hand, then the gentle lips brushed my fingers, and the horse picked up the apple delicately with her teeth and crunched it down.

"She's beautiful," I whispered, "and so gentle." I reached up again and softly stroked the velvety nose.

The other Land Girl had finished hitching Captain to the hay rake and they were clip-clopping towards the hay field.

"Come on, Sylvie," said Ruby. "Let's follow them and watch for a while, then I must take you back to your gran's house and get on with my work."

The horse and girl moved steadily into the field, and Ruby lifted me up to stand on a rung of the fence so I could see everything.

The combine harvester had worked around and around the field and now there was just a small patch of grass standing in the middle.

"Watch the edges of that patch of grass now, Sylvie," Ruby said, hanging on tight with her arm round my waist to keep me from falling.

The combine moved towards the last patch of grass, and the tall stems seemed to start moving and quivering all by themselves.

Rabbits! Rabbits were suddenly everywhere, bolting from the grass and running in all directions. The combine harvester had driven them into the middle of the field as they ran from its whirring blades, and now they had nowhere left to hide and had to break cover and run for their lives.

"It's a pity Mr Nailer's gone to market today," said Ruby, "or we'd be having rabbit pie for dinner!"

I loved rabbit pie, but seeing the soft brown rabbits running for freedom, I was glad that the farmer was away from the farm. This was their home, and what a beautiful place to live.

The sun was high in the sky now, and it was very hot. Talking about food made me feel suddenly hungry and tired, so I was glad when Ruby helped me down from the fence.

"Come on then," she said, brushing bits of straw from my dress and hair. "Let's get you back for your dinner."

"Not rabbit pie, though," I said, looking back at the baking field as we walked away.

"No, not today," agreed Ruby. "The rabbits live to fight another day." And she started singing, "Run, rabbit, run, rabbit run, run, run. . . ."

I joined in at the top of my voice and we sang all the way back to Grandma's house.

Chapter Five

Lessons Aren't Just For School

"Amy, you have remembered it's the church Flower Festival this weekend, haven't you?" asked Grandma when Mum came to pick us up one Wednesday in July.

"Yes, Grandma," replied Mum, "Mrs Fielding's having the girls tomorrow and Friday."

Oh! I'd forgotten that! We'd be spending the day at Maureen's house tomorrow! I liked going to Grandma's, but if we were just next door we could go home for any toys we wanted.

~*~

Instead of just popping through the hole in the fence, the next morning we went to Maureen's front door, like proper visitors. Audrey was a bit shy, and hung back, clinging to Mummy's cardigan, but when Mrs Fielding gave us all a slice of bread and marge sprinkled with hundreds and thousands, she settled down happily.

"Now then, girls, I need to go to the allotment and tidy up, so you can all come with me and play up there. Maureen, fetch your bucket and spade from the lean-to, Audrey can play with those where I can keep an eye on her, and you two can play anywhere on the allotments, BUT, you do NOT go out the gate, and if anyone you don't know talks to you, you come straight back to me, you understand?"

We nodded seriously.

~*~

The allotments were fun. There were paths between all the plots that we could run along, sheds to hide behind, sticks to play sword fighting with, and Mrs Fielding let us cut a length off a big reel of thick string from the shed so we could skip.

As the morning got hotter Maureen and I started to get tired, so we sat on the shed step in the shade and watched Audrey, who was making mud pies in the shade of the raspberry canes and chattering to herself the whole time.

Mrs Fielding gave us cucumber sandwiches and apples for our dinner, with a hard-boiled egg each, and a bottle of lemonade to share.

~*~

"What shall we do now?" asked Maureen, shaking the empty lemonade bottle up and down to make the marble stopper rattle.

"I don't know, what do you want to do?"

"It's too hot to run about, and I'm still hungry. Have you ever tried runner bean flowers?"

"Tried what with runner bean flowers?" I asked, puzzled. Maureen laughed until she fell over sideways on my lap.

"Eating them, silly!"

"You can't eat *flowers*!" I pushed her so she rocked back up again.

"Come on, try some." She jumped up and ran to the end of the allotment where the runner bean poles were, and picked off a handful of flowers. "Here, try."

I picked one out of her hand and nibbled it gingerly. It tasted just like runner beans, only softer and sweeter. I picked myself a handful and munched away.

~*~

"Girls! Where are you? I'm ready to go home. . . ."

Mrs Fielding crunched down the gravel path behind us and we heard a gasp.

"What have you done? My beans!"

"We only ate the flowers, Mum," said Maureen. "We didn't touch the beans."

Mrs Fielding's lips moved as though she was muttering to herself, and her eyes glinted. She looked like she was about to burst!

"The beans grow *from* the flowers, you silly girls! There won't *be* any beans now!"

"It was Sylvie's idea," lied Maureen. Sometimes I didn't like that girl one bit.

"I don't care whose idea it was, you are both in disgrace. Maureen, you are going straight to bed when you get home, and as for you, young lady, I will be speaking to your mother. You should know better, with your mum and dad working at the nurseries."

We trailed home miserably. I pinched Maureen's arm. "Liar! It was your idea."

"Was not!"

Audrey snivelled all the way home. I don't know what she'd got to cry about, she hadn't been told off!

~*~

Mum was already at home when Mrs Fielding knocked at our door. She looked at my dirty, tear-streaked face and folded her arms.

"I don't know what you've done to be told off, but I expect I'm about to find out. Go to your room, and take Audrey with you. I'll be up in a minute."

Mum came up the stairs slowly. I sat still on the bed, Audrey beside me, holding my hand and patting my knee, saying over and over, "Don't cwy, Sylvie."

Mum sat on the bed at the other side of me, with a creak of the springs.

"I'll have to tell your dad when he comes home. I don't know what he'll say. And you're not going round there tomorrow."

"It wasn't my idea, really, Mummy," I sniffed.

"I know." She gave me a hug. "That Maureen's a little liar, but she'll get her comeuppance one day. But, dearie, if you'd stopped and thought what you were doing before you followed her, you would have realised you shouldn't have eaten the flowers, wouldn't you?"

"Yes, Mummy. I just didn't think."

The front door opened and closed downstairs, and Daddy's voice called up the stairs "Hello? Anyone at home?"

Mum gave me a squeeze. "Stay here. I'll go and tell Daddy, and I'll call you down in a minute."

I could hear voices murmuring downstairs, but for once I didn't creep onto the stairs to hear better.

"Sylvia, come down here." Mum was calling.

I trailed down the stairs. Daddy was sitting in the armchair slowly filling his pipe. I stood in front of him.

"I'm sorry, Daddy. I know I shouldn't have picked Mrs Fielding's beans."

"We've got a bit of a problem here, haven't we, Ducks," said Daddy. "Mrs Fielding doesn't want to look after you tomorrow. She said she'll have Audrey, as she was the only one who behaved herself today, but you and Maureen are not to go out to play together for the rest of the week as punishment. Mummy and I both have to go to work, so it looks like you'll have to come with one of us."

I stood still and waited.

"You're going to come with me tomorrow, Sylvie," said Daddy, "but you won't be playing. I've got work for you to do!"

I looked up at him anxiously, but he was smiling a bit, so I felt slightly better.

"Now then, what's for my tea?"

Mum looked at me with a sideways smile. "Shepherd's pie and *our* runner beans."

~*~

It was very quiet when we left the house the next morning, it was so early. Daddy perched me on the carrier of his bike and

I hung on round his waist as he pedalled off. When we got to the start of the hill he said what he always said; "Breathe in, make yourself lighter, it's a long steep hill!"

At the bothy on the nursery, Daddy made us both a cup of tea, and then he sat me down on the step of the bothy and brought over a big wooden tub, which he filled with water, and another bucket full of dirty plant pots and wooden plant labels. He handed me a scrubbing brush.

"Here's your job for the morning. I want to see all these pots and labels scrubbed clean by dinner time, Cinderella." He winked. "If you need me, just shout, I'll just be over there digging the beds for the winter carrots."

~*~

At first it was quite fun, cleaning the pots and leaving them upside-down in the sun to dry, but it got really boring after a while. Daddy came back to the bothy to make another brew. "Is it dinner time yet?" I asked. Daddy laughed. "No Ducks, it's elevenses time. You can stop for a cuppa; you're doing a good job there."

Another hour to go!

The plant labels were easier to clean, and quite interesting, as I could read really well now I was nearly six, and I knew almost all the words on the labels, so I was quite surprised when Daddy came over and said it was dinner time.

"Because you've been such a good girl and done a really thorough job, I'm going to take you to the café for lunch. You can have a big tea with me when we get home tonight."

This day of being at work wasn't as bad as I thought it would be!

At the café, Daddy asked for tomato sandwiches. The bread was brown and crusty, the tomatoes were sweet and juicy, and after I watched Daddy lift the lid of his sandwich and shake salt and pepper on the tomatoes I did the same. It tasted wonderful!

~*~

"I've got another job for you this afternoon," said Daddy as we walked back to the nursery.

He set two big plant pots upside down with a board across the top beside the long bench in the potting house. He lifted me onto the board, so I could reach the bench, then he put a flat box full of soil in front of me, and a tray of tiny plants to the side of it.

He showed me how to pull the tiny plants out of the tray, very, very delicately, holding them by the leaf, not the stem, then make holes in the soil in the box with a little dibber, and gently place the tiny plants into the holes, firming the soil around them carefully.

He watched me while I slowly pricked out a whole row, then nodded.

"Good, Sylvie! We'll make a plantswoman of you yet. Carry on, I'm going back out to carry on digging the big bed. These are tiny baby carrots that you're pricking out. When they're a bit bigger they'll go out in the bed to grow nice and juicy for people to eat all winter."

I carried on working, but I was thinking hard all the time. It was slow, careful work pricking out those carrots. Someone else had already worked to grow them to the size they were, Daddy was working hard to prepare the bed for them, I was working as hard as I knew how . . . there was a lot of work involved in growing food, but it took just a second to pick something and eat it.

Now I understood why Mrs Fielding had been so angry with Maureen and me.

When Daddy came to tell me that it was time to go home, I was quiet and serious.

"Growing food is important, isn't it, Daddy?"

"Yes, Ducks, especially now there's a war on. A lot of the food we eat comes across the sea in ships, and we can't get that food now, because the German soldiers won't let the ships cross the sea, so everything we can grow here at home is really important."

He put his hand in his pocket and pulled out a shilling.

"Here are your wages, Sylvie, You've done a really good day's work today. You've earned this, and I think you've learned an important lesson, haven't you? What will you spend your shilling on?"

I tilted my hand and watched the sun shine on the coin.

"There's a shop here, isn't there, where people can buy plants?"

"Yes, there is. Do you want to buy something to grow in our garden?"

"No," I said, thoughtfully. "Can I buy a plant for Mrs Fielding? To say sorry?"

"Of course you can, Ducks. That's a really good idea." And he gave me a big hug.

Chapter Six

Fire Watching

We stumbled out of the shelter for the third time that night, Audrey grizzling, Mummy looking exhausted, and Daddy looking worried.

Scamp had decided it wasn't worth coming out and spent most of his nights in the shelter waiting for us to join him.

I'd soon learned to sleep through all the banging. "Blitzkrieg" it was called, which meant "lightning war", as we'd been told at school, and that's what it was like: a big loud thunder storm with crashes and flashes all round. This was the fifth night in a row that we'd had to head for the shelter.

Daddy looked at his watch. Four o'clock.

"Time for me to be on duty, Ducks," he said, giving Mummy a quick squeeze as she tried to soothe Audrey.

"You and Audrey go up to bed and try to get some rest; I'll take Sylvie with me. Those ba . . . bombers won't come back tonight, and if I take the picnic rug she can sleep on one of the benches in the bell loft."

Mum and Audrey trailed slowly up the stairs, and Daddy reached into the cupboard for our coats and his tin hat. He pulled on his armband with the letters FW for Fire Watcher painted on it and settled it over his overcoat sleeve.

He opened the front door and switched on the torch, carefully pointing its narrow beam of light at the ground. The piece of black card taped over the lamp let just enough light through so we could see where we were walking and not trip up, but not so much that any enemy planes overhead could spot the light.

We walked to the end of our road and crossed the silent main street over to the church.

The churchyard was very eerie at night; there was enough moonlight tonight to cast shadows of the big yew trees on the graves, so sometimes it looked as though the stones were moving. It had been moonlit for the last few nights, and the bombers had taken good advantage of the clear skies.

Daddy took a big iron key from his coat pocket and opened the door to the bell tower. There was a faint rustling noise and the gleam of little beady eyes in the dim torchlight as we made our way up the dark, twisty stairs and into the bell loft, where the five massive bells hung silent on their beams.

Pinned to the walls was a notice in large black letters; "The bells are not to be rung for the duration of the war, except in case of enemy invasion."

Daddy flopped the folded picnic rug down onto one of the wide benches that ran around the sides of the room, and led me over to one of the slatted windows. He helped me up onto the bench and, with his arm around my waist holding me safe, he pointed to the south east, where a golden glow lit up the night.

"You see that light, Sylvie?" he asked. "That's the fires in London, caused by all the bombs that have fallen."

I felt a prickly sensation at the back of my nose, like I was about to cry.

"Is everything burnt up?" I asked quietly. "All the buildings?"

"Not all, but a lot," said Daddy, sounding sad.

"I'll tell you a story, Sylvie," he said. "You'll learn about this at school soon, but I'll tell it the way I know it.

"About three hundred years ago, there was a terrible illness called the plague that killed a lot of people in London and across the country.

"When the plague was at its worst, something else happened that was terrible — a baker in London set fire to his shop by accident, and, because all the buildings in London were wooden back then, nearly everything was destroyed in a big fire that took hold of the whole city."

I held my breath, imagining how frightening that must have been.

"But," Daddy went on, "the fire killed all the germs that caused the plague and, after the fire, a very clever man called Sir Christopher Wren re-designed London, bigger and better. One of the things he built is St Paul's Cathedral. Do you remember when we took you to the pantomime that Christmas when you were three and we passed St Paul's Cathedral on the bus?"

Oh yes! I remembered the big square building with the dome on the top. It had been full of light and music, and the bells were ringing into the cold air. I remembered how silly I had been when I was younger; I had thought it was Buckingham Palace!

Daddy continued his story, "Well, St Paul's is still standing. It's a bit battered around the edges, but it's still there, in the middle of all those fires, just like us. We're in the middle of a war and we're still here.

"And d'you know what? Even if it was completely destroyed, it doesn't matter. Things made by people can be made again, but people can't. It's people that matter, not buildings or property."

We stood silently, watching the fire burning far away.

"Now then, I'd better get on with my job, and you, young lady, need to bed down on that bench and get some kip."

He tucked me in under the picnic rug and for a while I watched him moving slowly and quietly about the bell tower, looking out across the village below, watching for fires; smaller fires than the one raging in London, but just as deadly.

~*~

I must have fallen asleep, as the next thing I knew was a clump of boots on the stairs, and a man appeared at the door wearing a tin hat and a FW armband, just like Daddy.

"Morning, Jack," said Daddy. "All quiet now. Hopefully, it'll stay that way and give us a bit of peace."

Jack nodded, smiled at me, and unpacked a small tin box that contained a packet of bread and butter. "Breakfast," he grinned, and tucked in, his elbows on the window sill, looking out of the slatted window across the village.

As we emerged from the heavy door at the bottom of the tower, the sun was coming up.

"Let's go home and take Mummy a cup of tea in bed. I'll help you make it for her."

The house was quiet. Scamp had decided to come in and was sleeping in a coil on the rug. We tiptoed into the kitchen and Daddy filled the kettle and set it on the stove to boil, keeping a careful eye on it so he could take it off before it whistled.

I took a cup and saucer from the sideboard and set it on a tray, very carefully, so as not to make any chinking noise.

I spooned tea into the pot, one for Mummy, one for Daddy, and one for the pot, and Daddy carefully poured the boiling water onto the leaves.

We sat quietly at the table, watching the sun rise over the garden while the tea brewed. Another day, and we'd survived another bad night.

Daddy poured the tea into the cup, added some milk powder and stirred. He carried the tray carefully upstairs as I tiptoed behind, then he opened the door to the front bedroom and handed me the tray.

I carried it ever so carefully across the room and put it down on the bedside table. Mummy was still sleeping, so I gently tapped her shoulder, then leaned over and kissed her cheek. She woke slowly and smiled at me.

"I brought you a cup of tea." I whispered. Audrey was still sleeping.

"Oh, such a good girl!" smiled Mum, and reached out for her glasses. Her hand clipped the edge of the teacup and, disaster! The cup tipped over and tea spilt all over the tray.

"Oh, darling, I'm so sorry," she cried softly. "All your hard work."

I looked at Daddy and smiled. I knew what to say.

"Don't worry, Mummy, it's just a thing. Things made by people can be made again."

Chapter Seven

An Angel and A Visitor

The low winter sun was slanting through the high windows of classroom two on the first day back after the half term holiday, and the whole of Class Two was fidgety after an energetic lunch hour.

"Listen, please, everyone." Miss Hills raised her voice over the noise of chatter and scraping chairs and waited for quiet.

"We only have six weeks left of the school term, and it will be the first of November on Friday, so we are going to start preparing for the Christmas Nativity play."

Everyone sat just a little straighter in their chair.

"This afternoon, I am going to read you the story of Jesus' birth, which I hope you all know, as a reminder of what our play is about, and then I want you to draw a picture of the stable in Bethlehem in your Scripture books. Tomorrow morning, there will be a special assembly where Miss Manning will announce the names of the people who are going to play Mary, Joseph, and the Three Kings."

I sat back in my chair and let my mind drift away while Miss Hills read the story from the Children's Bible. I knew the story. I was six years old now and had been going to Sunday school for ages. Well, two months, anyway.

I started daydreaming about playing the part of the Virgin Mary, wearing a blue robe and riding on a donkey. Maybe there would be a real donkey! Last year, I had been a lamb in the Nativity play. They never let the first years have proper parts with words to say.

"So, that's the story," said Miss Hills, closing the big book. "Let me see how well you can draw the stable scene."

Desk lids creaked and pencil cases were opened. Mummy and Daddy had given me a brand new set of Rowney Victoria pencils for my birthday, and I took great care not to drop them and break the leads.

As we worked at our drawings, Maureen suddenly announced, "I'm going to play the Virgin Mary." I put my pencil down and stared at her.

"No, you're not!" I said indignantly. "Miss said Miss Manning's going to tell us tomorrow who's going to be who, so you can't already know."

"I don't *know*," said Maureen mysteriously, "but I bet you I will be Mary."

She smiled smugly, slid out of her chair and went to the front of the room to speak to Miss Hills. Whatever she was saying, Miss Hills seemed to find it very interesting. I frowned and went back to colouring in my drawing of a donkey.

~*~

When I knocked for Maureen the next morning, she came out of her house with a bundle under her arm, wrapped in brown paper and tied with a string.

"What's that?" I asked, poking it.

"Don't touch!" she squealed. "It's a secret. Mum said I wasn't to show anyone."

I stuck my tongue out at her. "Don't tell then. Keep your secret. I didn't want to know, anyway."

As we queued up to go into Assembly, Maureen handed her paper-wrapped bundle to Miss Hills, who nodded and tucked it away in the paper cupboard.

~*~

The hall buzzed with excitement, and Miss Manning had to call for quiet a few times before everyone was silent. Anxious faces stared up at her as she began to call out the names of children who would have the star parts in the play.

". . .and the Virgin Mary will be played by . . . Maureen Fielding from Class Two."

I couldn't believe my ears! That parcel must have had something to do with it! Maybe it was a cake! Yes, that was it, she'd given Miss Hills a cake as a bribe to get the part! And I bet it was a black market cake, too! I wasn't sure how a market could be black, and why you'd want to eat the food from there if it was black too, but anything that was nice and extra tasty seemed to be from there.

Maureen primped smugly and tossed her golden-brown curls around her shoulders.

"Told you so," she whispered, and nudged me in the ribs. I don't know whether it was her smug voice or the nudge that made me feel hot all over, but before I realised what I'd done I pinched her arm, hard.

"Ow!" she squeaked, rubbing the place where I'd pinched her. I saw Miss Manning's head turn in our direction and hissed at Maureen to be quiet.

"And now," said Miss Manning, "I want the five children whose names I call out next to line up outside my office. The rest of you may go back to your classrooms."

Everyone looked around as Miss Manning started to call out the names, wondering what those children had done to be sent to the headmistress' office.

When *my* name was called I knew. I'd been seen pinching Maureen's arm.

I trailed slowly to the office and sat on the bench outside with the other four children. They were looking at each other nervously, but I just kept my head down and looked at my feet. I'd be in such trouble when I got home.

Miss Manning's shoes clicked over the parquet floor and she stopped in front of us.

"Don't look so miserable, you five," she laughed, "you're not in trouble. I understand from your class teachers that you are the best readers in the school, and I want to hear you all read to me, so I can choose one of you to be the Angel Gabriel in the play. It's a very important part, as the angel has a lot of words to learn, so it has to be played by one of the very best readers in the school."

One by one we were called into the office to read from a sheet of paper the words that the Angel Gabriel says to the shepherds. They were lovely words, like a poem, only they didn't rhyme. I didn't understand all of what I read, but I liked the way it sounded.

As each of us finished reading we were told to wait outside until Miss Manning had heard everyone read.

She followed the last child back into the corridor and looked at us all in turn.

"Well, I am *very* impressed with all of you. You have all shown a very high standard of reading, but I am going to give the part to the child who put the most feeling into the reading, and that was Sylvia Ford. Well done, Sylvia, this is a very important part, and you are still only a second year! Now, I want you to take these lines home and practice and practice. You need to learn them by heart, and you need to say them loud enough for everyone in the hall to be able to hear you. Do you think you can do that?"

"Oh, yes, Miss! Thank you, Miss!"

I almost skipped back to the classroom.

Maureen looked at me eagerly when I walked in. "Did she give you lines?" she asked, with that same smug look on her face.

"Yes, she did," I said and shoved the sheet of paper under her smug nose. "The Angel Gabriel's lines! And I bet my halo will be bigger than yours!"

~*~

I ran through the back door calling out, "Mum, Mum, guess what? I'm going to be the Angel Gabriel in the school play, and I have to learn all these words. . . ."

I stopped dead in the kitchen door. There was a strange man sitting on the settee, with Audrey perched on his knee and

Scamp sitting at his feet. A very tall man with wild curly black hair and twinkly blue eyes.

"Well, now, this pretty colleen must be your older daughter, Mrs Ford."

"My name's not Colleen, it's Sylvie!" I cried. "Who are you?"

"Sylvia, remember your manners," said Mum gently. "Do you remember Auntie Kattie?"

I nodded. Auntie Kattie wasn't a real auntie, we just called her that. Before I was born, Mum worked for a rich family in a big house, and Auntie Kattie had worked there as the cook. I hadn't seen her for a while, as Mum said she had gone back to live in Ireland where she came from, but I remembered her visiting when I was younger, before Audrey was born, and I remembered the smell of Yardley talc when I sat on her lap.

"Well," Mum went on, "this is Auntie Kattie's son Micky. He's come to England to find a job and he's staying here for a few days."

Micky stood up and came over to shake my hand, just like I was a grown up, and I noticed that he was even taller than I'd imagined, and walked with a very bad limp.

"Oh! What happened to your leg?" I asked.

"Sylvie!" Mum scolded.

"It's all right, Mrs Ford, I don't mind telling her."

He crouched down in front of me, slowly, easing his bad leg, and looked at me solemnly. "I used to work in a circus, on the high wire, until one day. . . ." He made walking movements in the air with his fingers and then let his hand fall, making a slow, falling whistling noise. "So you see, I have this bad leg, and they won't have me in the army, so I need to find another job to do."

I heard Mum make a smothered noise, as though she was laughing, but it wasn't anything to laugh about! The poor man!

"I hope you find a job soon, and I hope it's one where you can sit down!" I said.

Micky burst out laughing at that, and just then Daddy came through the door and shook Micky warmly by the hand.

Mum called to me to help her set the table for tea, and we all took our seats.

"So, did young Maureen get to be the Virgin Mary?" asked Daddy as he dished up the potatoes.

I gazed at him open mouthed. "How did you know?" I asked.

"Mrs Fielding came round the other night, after you and Audrey were in bed, to ask Mummy to help her mend the costume she wore when she was Mary in *her* school play, so she could give it to Maureen to wear."

So that was what was in the parcel! And Maureen only got the part because she already had the costume!

I told Daddy about being given the Angel Gabriel's lines to learn, and what Miss Hills had said about learning them by heart and saying them loud.

"I can help ye with that," said Micky, after tea. "You stand at the top of the stairs and read those lines at the top of your voice. I'll stand in the kitchen and see if I can hear ye, then we'll do it line by line until you know the whole thing. You're a clever little colleen, ye'll have it by heart in no time."

~*~

The day of the Christmas play arrived.

The performance was due to start at half past five, so the parents who worked could come and see the play. All of us who were actors stayed behind after school finished and were given a tea of egg sandwiches and bread and jam, served up to us by the mothers who were helping us get dressed in our costumes. I was doubly excited, I not only had a really good part, but my new friend Micky was coming to see me act! He had only stayed with us for a week, and had found a job and lodgings in another village, but he always managed to pop round on a Sunday afternoon at tea time. He said the walk helped keep his bad leg from seizing up, and he always brought something nice for

Audrey and me; a bird's feather he'd found, a picture postcard, and one day a little wooden whistle he'd made himself.

He would sit at the kitchen table and tell us stories about his days in the circus, which for some reason always made Mum laugh and shake her head.

Behind the curtain, on the little stage made of upside down bread crates and boards, I could hear the audience filing into the hall, chattering and laughing. I straightened my gold tinsel halo, and swished the long skirt of my white angel's dress. I liked my costume much better than Maureen's, and mine was new! Made specially for me from one of Mummy's old sheets.

Miss Manning laid a cool hand on my shoulder and whispered "Good luck!" with a smile, then stepped though the curtain onto the front of the stage to welcome the parents. I slipped back into the wings to watch the first part of the play where Mary and Joseph were trying to find somewhere to stay. Maureen didn't have one word to say, not one! Joseph did all the talking in their part of the play.

Then it was my turn! I climbed carefully up the three steps of the small stepladder placed at the back of the stage. There was a battery lantern hanging from a beam in the ceiling, and as I started to speak my lines Miss Hills would switch it on so it looked as though the light was shining from my halo.

The curtains opened and I started to speak my lines.

"Fear not, for behold. . . ." But the light didn't come on! Miss Hills reached up to the switch and flicked it on and off, but nothing happened. She tried to reach up to unhook the lantern, but she was too small, and the lantern was too high, and she couldn't stand on the stepladder because I was standing on it.

Suddenly a soft voice whispered "Don't worry, ladies, I can fix this!"

Micky!

He reached up a long arm, fiddled with something on the back of the lantern and the light came on!

I beamed almost as brightly as the light and began again.
"Fear not, for behold, I bring you glad tidings of great joot;..."

Chapter Eight

Christmas

"It's just not right, not hearing church bells on Christmas morning," sighed Mum as she slid Audrey's porridge bowl across the table to her. "I don't mind on Sundays, I've got used to it, I suppose, and I can definitely do without Thursday evening bell practice, but Christmas Day. . . ." She sat down carefully, arranging her apron over the lap of her best dress.

We were going to Grandma's for dinner, and as there were no buses it would be a long walk, so Mum had already had her bath and dressed, to leave time for the rest of us to get ready.

"They should make a special ring for Christmas Day," I said, through a mouthful of porridge. "A tune that says:

The Germans haven't invaded, we're okay,
We're just ringing bells for Christmas Day."

I chanted it in a sing song voice.

Everyone burst out laughing, including Audrey, who was too little to remember the church bells ringing before the war.

~*~

We waited at the gate while Daddy locked the door, Audrey bouncing in the pram, which she had really outgrown. She was coming three now, but it was too far for her to walk to Grandma's, and uphill most of the way, so Mum would push her, and I would ride on the seat of Daddy's bike while he wheeled it alongside the pram. Scamp walked. He didn't like it, but he walked.

I had been disappointed when I woke up and saw that there was no snow, but now the thought of struggling up the hill to Grandma's slipping and sliding made me quite glad that it was dry.

The door opened at Grandma's and there was Auntie Mabel, smiling and holding her arms out for a hug! As I kissed her and she exclaimed at how big I was, I could hear other voices from the kitchen, and there were the other aunties, Maude and Maggie, running across the room to hug us, and tease Auntie Mabel that she wasn't the youngest in the house any more.

The "three Ms" pulled us into the house and helped us out of our coats, chatting all the time, while Scamp danced around, barking.

Audrey was a bit shy at first. She knew Auntie Maude, as she worked at Park Grange House just up the hill, and was at home on her days off, but Auntie Maggie worked for a family in London, and only came home when she had a week off, and Auntie Mabel was a nursery maid with a family who lived all the way down by the sea, just across from the Isle of Wight, so she hardly ever came home.

Auntie Mabel had promised me that when I was big enough to go on the train by myself I could travel down and stay with her, and she would take me to the seaside and on the boat over to the Isle of Wight. I made a note to myself to remember to ask her after dinner whether I was big enough yet.

The house smelt wonderful! Chicken, potatoes, and a fruity smell that I hoped was Christmas pudding. Grandma had huge jars of dried fruit in her larder cupboard, I knew, as she sometimes gave me a small handful of raisins to eat if I was very good, so I hoped she'd saved enough for a pudding.

Daddy had escaped from all the hugging and giggling and slipped past his sisters into the kitchen, where he was helping Grandma lift the roasting tin out of the oven. It was a big bird, but it wouldn't go far among all of us, so it was just as well that not all the uncles would be here!

Grandma wiped her hands on her apron and came to give us all a hug. "Is Uncle Johnny here, Grandma?" I asked when she released me from her squeaky kisses.

"Yes, dear, he's just popped next door to see Mrs Brownlow. He'll be back in a minute, and I had a postcard from your Uncle Arthur to say he'll be here in time for tea; he managed to get a four-day pass and he's walking over from his friend Bert's at Woodfield. At least he is if he managed to get the train from London."

A sudden gust of cold air blew in through the back door, bringing with it Uncle Johnny, looking much older than I remembered, and somehow taller in his sailor's whites.

He beamed when he saw us and hugged us all round, tickling Audrey and making her fall about giggling. When he kissed me, I smelt a warm, spicy smell, and Grandma must have noticed it too, as she leaned over me and sniffed.

"Hmmm. . . . Mrs Brownlow's had the sherry bottle open, I see," she said icily.

"It's Christmas Day, Ma," said Uncle Johnny. "And besides, I'm in the navy now. Can you imagine if I turned down my daily ration of rum?" He winked at me.

Daddy patted his youngest brother on the back. "I think I'll just pop next door and wish Mrs Brownlow compliments of the season. . . ."

"Oh, no, you will not, Thomas, you'll get yourself into the front room and help your sisters put the extra leaves in the table, then you can sharpen that carving knife for me."

Daddy laughed and rolled up his sleeves.

"Come on, girls," said Mum, "out of Grandma's way. Go and help Auntie Mabel get the knives and forks out." She unhooked Grandma's spare apron from behind the door and went to help with the cooking.

~*~

We had just finished laying the table when there was a knock at the door. I ran to open it, and there were Auntie Dot with my cousin Edie, and Auntie Hattie with my cousins Pamela and John.

Edie was skipping with excitement "Daddy's coming home, he'll be here for tea, then he's coming home with us for three days before goes back to the war!"

I was looking forward to seeing Uncle Arthur. He was big and jolly, but I hoped he'd manage not to upset Auntie Maggie; they always ended up arguing. Daddy said it was all just fun, and they'd been like that since they were small children, but I didn't like it when Auntie Maggie shouted.

"Come on," called John, who was a year younger than me, but reckoned he was in charge because he was a boy, "let's go upstairs and play in the cave!"

"Have you asked Grandma if you can go upstairs?" asked Auntie Hattie, weakly. "Oh, dear . . . don't break anything, children!"

We thumped off up the stairs, with Audrey lagging behind, to play in our favourite place in the house, the "cave" under Grandma's big high iron bedstead.

"Let them be, Hattie," said Auntie Dot as we disappeared around the corner of the stairs, Scamp chasing our heels. "The quicker they tire themselves out, the better they'll sleep."

~*~

Christmas dinner was a feast! We all ate as much as we could manage, if not more. As Auntie Dot said, "You wouldn't think there was a war on!"

"It's all legal, Dorothy", said Grandma sharply. "I don't have any dealings with black market things."

I saw Daddy glance sideways at Mum with a slight smile, as he speared the last sausage onto his fork. We'd brought the sausages; Mum had sent me down to the butcher at the end of the road to get them, taking a bottle of wine made from our gooseberries. She said I had to wait until there was no-one in the shop before I went in, as otherwise they'd all want some gooseberry wine, and we didn't have enough for the whole village.

When the last spoon clattered into the last empty bowl, my cousin Pamela piped up, "Thank you, God, for my good food. Please, Grandma, may I get down?"

Grandma wiped her lips delicately and folded her napkin. "Yes, dear, but don't run about until your dinner's gone down."

One by one, the other cousins said Grace and asked to leave the table. Even Audrey made a stab at saying it and was allowed to climb down. I looked down at my plate and swung my feet under the table.

"Don't you want to go and play, Sylvie?" asked Auntie Maggie.

"Yes, Duck, run and play," said Daddy with a nudge.

I started to slide down from my chair, but Grandma's voice froze me on the spot.

"Don't you have something to say first, Sylvia?"

I squirmed. "Thank-you-God-for-my-good-food-please-Grandma-may-I-get-down?" I gabbled.

I hated having to say that; I was grateful for my dinner and everything, it was just that it was impossible to say it like you meant it unless you got in first, and there was no chance of that with goody-goody Pam around.

"You may, dear," said Grandma, and I ran away eagerly.

~*~

A knock at the door and a burst of laughter from the grown-ups sent Edie flying down the stairs, jumping the last two completely to be caught up in a big hug by Uncle Arthur, and was the signal for Grandma and the three Ms to head for the kitchen to put the kettle on and make sandwiches for tea.

Over tea, the uncles and Daddy talked seriously about the war, until Auntie Maggie said "Oh, dry up, Arthur!" and started one of their spats.

"Come on, Arthur," said Daddy, "let's set the dartboard up in the scullery and have a game. Are you coming, Johnny? And all you kids, you can pick up the darts your Uncle Arthur misses with!"

~*~

It was cold in the scullery, so our mothers insisted on wrapping us up warmly in scarves and shawls. Auntie Mabel came out with us, to make sure none of us strayed into the line of fire.

Daddy set up the dartboard on the back of the door and chalked two long lines on a blackboard that hung on the wall at the other end of the room, then he wrote T, A and J at the top of the three columns he'd made.

"Here you are, Sylvie." He handed me the chalk. "Write 501 at the top of each of those columns, and when each of us calls out a number, you take that number away from five hundred and one, and write the answer under it, then the next time you take the next number away from that answer. Got it? Let's see how good you are at sums!"

The men played one long game right down to the last double one that Uncle Arthur insisted on throwing to clear his score, even though he'd been beaten by his brothers.

"Why don't you have a go, kids?" said Uncle Johnny. "Play a game with Auntie Mabel. We're just going to pop out for a bit."

"John!" protested Auntie Mabel, as the men buttoned up their coats and slipped out the back door.

"Don't worry," winked Uncle Johnny. "While those darts are hitting the back of that door, no-one's going to come through it, are they!"

~*~

We played really badly at first, but after Auntie Mabel moved the dartboard down a bit we started to get the hang of it, and surprisingly, Pam was the best of all of us.

Auntie Mabel seemed worried, though. She kept looking at her watch, and she obviously wasn't concentrating, as she kept getting the score wrong.

Suddenly, we heard footsteps and laughter on the path outside and the men were back. They all looked very rosy-cheeked and jolly, and laughed at the relief on Auntie Mabel's face.

"Come on then, kids, time to go and hear what His Majesty has to say to us," said Uncle Johnny, reaching for the scullery door handle, but Auntie Mabel was faster, and pushed him gently back with her hand on his shoulder. "Not until you've all had a peppermint," she said, pulling a small tin from her cardigan pocket. Uncle Johnny grinned and took one. Of course, all us kids wanted a sweet too, so we burst back into the kitchen with a waft of peppermint, just as Grandma turned the wireless on to listen to the King's Christmas Broadcast.

I snuggled on the settee next to Mum, feeling suddenly tired from all the food and excitement, and I must have dozed off. As I woke up, the King was just finishing his speech in that odd jerky way of speaking that he had.

"And now I wish you all a happy Christmas and a happier New Year. We may look forward to it with sober confidence. We have surmounted a grave crisis. We do not underrate the dangers and difficulties which confront us still, but we take courage and comfort from the successes which our fighting men and their Allies have won at heavy odds by land and air and sea.

"The future will be hard, but our feet are planted on the path of victory, and with the help of God we shall make our way to justice and to peace."

Chapter Nine

We'll Take A Cup of Kindness

I couldn't tell which was making the most noise, the stew bubbling on the stove, or my stomach rumbling.

As I laid the table, Audrey was running round and round it, shouting "Happy New Ears!" and laughing. She knew it was Happy New Year really, but she thought ears was funnier. It was, the first hundred times.

It was very late to be waiting for tea, nearly ten o'clock, and way past my bedtime and Audrey's, but we'd had a nap in the afternoon, and didn't get up again until eight. Mum said there was no point in making us go to bed, as we'd only get up and sit on the stairs when the singing started.

A knock at the front door sent Mum rushing into the front room, wiping her hands on a tea towel, to let Mrs Fielding and Maureen in. Mrs Fielding was carrying a cake tin, and Maureen had a bottle that looked like ginger beer.

"The stew's all ready and waiting," said Mum, smiling. "Come through to the kitchen and sit down. Tom, can you open a bottle of the best peapod and pour for Mrs Fielding, please?" She winked at Mrs Fielding and handed her a small wine glass.

"Don't mind if I do, Mrs Ford." Mrs Fielding chuckled as the golden wine tinkled into her glass.

We sat up to the table, Audrey now on a chair; she'd grown out of her high chair, but she still needed three cushions to bring her up to the level of the table.

Daddy tapped his knife on his wine glass after we were all seated.

"Before we eat, a toast," he said, looking suddenly serious. "We've made it through another year of war, we're all alive and well, in good health, and getting on with life as best we can. Let's raise a glass; you too, girls; to absent friends, and health and happiness in 1941."

We all raised our glasses. Audrey slopped a little of her lemonade, but for once no-one was worried. "Absent friends, and health and happiness in 1941," we chorused.

"Nineteen formty wump" echoed Audrey.

Laughter broke out around the table and we tucked in to our stew. It was more vegetable than meat, as usual, but it tasted wonderful!

"Come on then, everyone, gather round the piano," called Daddy, after the washing up was dried and put away. "What shall it be? Mrs F? Do you want to choose the first song?"

"Let's start with some of the old songs from the last war," she said, her fingers dancing over the keys, making trills and runs. "We all know Tipperary, don't we?" she nodded at Maureen and me.

We knew that one! We sang it at school in music lessons.

"All together then," cried Mrs Fielding, vamping with her left hand and counting us in with her right.

"It's a long waaaaay to Tipperareeeeee. . . ," we started, and when we finished the verse and chorus Mum called "Again!" and we began round again, but Mum and Mrs Fielding sang Pack Up Your Troubles while the rest of us carried on with Tipperary, and the two songs fitted perfectly together! We sang it once more, then Maureen lost her place and started singing the wrong song to the wrong tune, and it all fell apart with gales of laughter.

Daddy took down the Community Song Book from the top of the piano, and, with a sly glance at Mum, opened it at The Ash Grove.

"Oh, Tom. . . ," Mum protested, but Audrey and I grabbed

her hands and swung them, shouting "Yes! Sing The Ash Grove!"

Mum hung her head and looked shy, but Mrs Fielding played the first line and nudged her with her elbow, and they grinned at each other.

Mum's lovely alto voice ran up and down the old tune with its sad story and beautiful words, and when she ended the song we all stood silent for a minute. Mrs Fielding wiped the corner of her eye with a finger, and Daddy cleared his throat.

"How about the Lincolnshire Poacher?" he asked, breaking the silence, and Mrs Fielding launched into the rumpty-tumpty-tum rhythm of the lively tune.

In the middle of it being "a shiny night in the season of the year" we heard an ominous sound; the air raid siren.

"Oh! I knew you should have come to us!" cried Mrs Fielding. "Come on, Maureen, we need to get home."

"Nonsense," exclaimed Daddy, "our shelter's not big, but there's room for two little 'uns!"

"Oh, no!" Mrs Fielding panicked, "I can't be doing with enclosed spaces! I want to get in the Morrison!"

Mum sighed impatiently. We could have had a Morrison shelter in our kitchen, but Mum had said she'd be blowed if she got rid of our nice oak table, that was her mum's, and have that nasty cage pretending to be a table plonked in the middle of the floor. She didn't care whether it was safe, it was ugly. Our shelter would go outside.

"Don't be silly," she snapped. "You can't go out while this is going on. Can't you hear the planes? If you won't come in the shelter with us, then at least get in the cupboard under the stairs."

Mrs Fielding ushered Maureen into the cupboard, but left the door open. Scamp darted in behind them, hoping for cuddles, while the rest of us scuttled out of the lean-to door and down the shelter steps.

We sat in silence for a while, listening to the "whump, whump" of the engines of the bomber planes flying overhead. Even on New Year's Eve, the war was going on. I remembered Daddy telling me about the British and German soldiers stopping fighting and playing football on Christmas Day during the last war. If they could be friends on Christmas Day why couldn't they be friends all the time? Sometimes adults made no sense at all.

"Let's go on singing," said Daddy, bouncing Audrey on his knee. "You can count to ten, can't you, Audrey? How about Ten Green Bottles?" Audrey clapped her hands and shouted "Ten Gween Bockles!" So we started singing.

The ninth green bottle didn't get a chance to fall when the All Clear sounded, and we trooped back indoors to find Maureen and her mum sitting at the kitchen table, a little dusty and cobwebby, but calmer.

"Oooh, I'm glad that's over," said Mrs Fielding, shuddering. "I hate the sound of those planes."

The clock in the front room made the clearing-its-throat noise it always made when it was about to strike, and Daddy looked at his pocket watch. "Midnight! Fill your glasses, everyone!"

Just then there was a loud knock at the front door.

"Oh no!" Mum groaned theatrically, "I bet that's the Warden. There must have been a chink of light showing in the front window." She threw an odd glance, almost a wink, over her shoulder to Daddy, and swiftly crossed the front room to open the door.

We stood waiting, expecting the stern words, "Put that light out!" from Mr Chadwick, the Air Raid Warden for our street, but instead we heard a lilting voice cry out, "First footer, Mrs F!" and a tall, curly haired figure appeared in the hall, with a glass of something in one hand, and a lump of what looked like coal in the other. Micky!

I ran across the room and hugged him round the waist. He handed the glass to Daddy, and the lump of coal to Mum, with a deep formal bow, then swung me up in the air so my head nearly touched the ceiling. Scamp was barking with excitement at seeing his friend again.

"What's in the glass?" asked Maureen. I could tell she wanted to be thrown up to the ceiling too, but Micky didn't know her, so she had to get his attention by being nosy.

"'Tis a drop of the good stuff, real Irish whiskey," Micky replied.

"Irish tradition says that if the first person to visit a house on New Year's Day is a dark-haired man, bringing whisky and coal, good luck will be with the household all year."

Dad tilted the glass of whiskey in a silent toast to Micky and sipped, then handed the glass back to him.

"Ladies first," said Micky, passing the glass to Mum with a smile. Mum took a delicate sip, just wetting her lips with the golden liquid, smiled, and handed the glass to Mrs Fielding, who took a deep swig, gasped and choked.

"Can we try?" Maureen begged.

"Just a tiny bit," answered Daddy. "You and Sylvie may each have a sip, but just a sip!"

Maureen grabbed the glass greedily and tipped it to her mouth. "Euuuurrghhh!" she spluttered. "That's awful!"

The adults laughed, and I determined to take my sip without making as much fuss as Maureen. I'd pretend it was castor oil.

I took a sip and swallowed slowly. It tasted cold first, then suddenly warm, and I could feel it going all the way down, settling warmly in my stomach. It felt odd, but good!

"Oh!" I gasped in surprise, looking up at Micky.

"Sure and ye're a natural whiskey drinker, my little colleen," he laughed.

He knelt on the rug and swung a drawstring bag down from his shoulder.

"Let's see what we have in here, shall we?" His blue eyes twinkled as he opened the bag.

He pulled out two tiny velvet bags, and handed one to me and one to Maureen. Inside each was a silky green cord, and hung from each cord was a tiny enamel four-leafed clover.

"A lucky Irish shamrock," Micky explained, as he hung them around our necks.

He stood up and dug in the bag again, pulling out two small boxes. He handed one each to Mum and Mrs Fielding, and rummaged in the bag once more.

"Oh!" gasped Mum, opening her box. Inside, nestled on a little velvet cushion, was a beautiful glass paperweight with a real shamrock leaf set into the base. Mrs Fielding's box held the same.

How had he known to bring presents for Maureen and her mum?

He was magical!

The last item in the bag was for Daddy. A small bottle of golden liquid. Whiskey!

Daddy shook Micky warmly by the hand, and took down another small glass from the cupboard in the corner. He poured in a tot of the whiskey, topped up Micky's glass, and the peapod wine for Mum and Mrs Fielding, and re-filled Maureen's glass and mine with ginger beer.

We all suddenly remembered Audrey and looked around for her. She was curled up on the settee, fast asleep, with Scamp curled up on her feet.

"She can have her gift in the morning," said Micky, as he picked up Mummy's cardigan from the arm of the settee and tucked it around the sleeping Audrey.

We stood in a circle in the middle of the floor, and all raised our glasses.

"Wishing blessings on this house and all within it, for the year to come, and ever more," said Micky. "Happy New Year!"

"Happy New Year!" we all replied, happily.

Micky's clear tenor voice lifted, and the adults joined in with a song I'd never heard before, both sweet and sad at the same time.

"Should auld acquaintance be forgot and never brought to mind. . . ."

Part Three
1941

Chapter Ten

Bottletops for Battleships

"Before I wish you a safe and happy Whitsun half-term holiday," said Miss Manning, "I have an announcement to make. Those of you who listen to the news broadcasts will know that our navy has suffered some bad losses in the last two years. Mr Churchill and the government have written to all the schools in Britain to ask the help of all the children in the country."

She paused, to make sure that we were listening intently.

"What Mr Churchill wants you to do, during half term, is to collect as many metal bottletops as you can. They will be used to raise money for a new battleship. You can collect on your own, or in pairs or groups, but whoever collects the most bottletops by the time we come back to school will be presented with a certificate, in a special assembly. You can ask your friends, family, and neighbours for as many bottletops as they can give you." She smiled. "Now, off you go, have a safe and happy holiday, and good luck!"

Maureen and I glanced sideways at each other. "Hodson's Alley," she muttered, and pinched the back of my hand. "Hodson's Alley," I replied, nodding, and pinched her back. The hand-pinch was our secret signal that meant, "We don't talk about this in front of anyone else".

As soon as we were let out of school, we ran as fast as we could to the dead-end alley that ran along the back of our row of houses, and finished behind the sweetshop. We knew that the boys from the big school sometimes gathered at the back of the shop to drink beer and smoke cigarettes, and they always threw their beer bottletops on the ground.

We were in luck! We rummaged through the leaves, fag ends and litter and collected up over a dozen bottletops, getting our hands filthy along the way. After a short argument about who should look after the bottletops overnight, I said goodbye to Maureen and ran home with my grimy loot.

I burst through the back door and scattered our collection across the kitchen table.

"Look, Mum! Maureen and me are going to win the certificate! We've got a dozen bottletops already!"

Mum stood, hands on hips, looking at the mess on her tablecloth.

"And they're going straight in the dustbin!" she said, angrily, reaching for the dustpan.

"Oh, no! You can't do that!" I cried, grabbing up my treasures. "Mr Churchill wants them! He's going to build a battleship out of them!"

Mum looked at me hard, and her mouth twitched. I wasn't sure whether she was trying not to laugh or not to cry.

She took out a bucket from under the sink and silently half-filled it with water.

"Throw them in there, and put the bucket in the lean-to, then go and get a clean tablecloth from the sideboard. You can explain what this nonsense is about over tea when Daddy gets home; there's no point in saying it twice."

~*~

". . .so Mr Churchill wants all of us schoolkids to collect metal bottletops so he can build a battleship out of them," I finished, through the last mouthful of suet pudding.

"Hmm. . . ." said Daddy, filling his pipe slowly and thoughtfully, "I don't think he's going to get much of a battleship out of twelve or thirteen bottletops!"

Mum laughed, "She should go and see old Sid Bryant down the road; I bet he's got a few bottletops stashed away!"

"Amy. . . ." said Dad, in a warning tone of voice.

"Oh, old Sid's harmless," said Mum, collecting the plates and piling them one on top of the other. Daddy hated it when she did that, because all the left-over gravy went on the clean bottoms of the plates on top, so she always did it on purpose, ending at Daddy's place with a stack of plates, wiggling them to make sure the gravy was well spread, and winking at him.

"Sid's no trouble, he's just usually three sheets to the wind," she said as she carried the plates to the sink.

Mr Bryant down the road was a bit scary. He had a very red face, and he didn't always talk sense, and sometimes he seemed to have trouble walking, so all us kids stayed away from him.

I didn't really understand what Mum meant about the sheets, though; Mr Bryant's garden backed on to the school field and all I'd ever seen on his washing line was a load of grey vests and long johns.

I clattered down the stairs the next morning, with my nice clean bottletops in my gym-shoes bag. I'd slept with them under the bed in case anyone tried to break in and steal them. This was vital war work, that's why I hadn't wanted to trust Maureen to keep them safe; they didn't have a dog next door. Not that Scamp was a very good guard dog; he spent most of his time in the Fieldings' garden digging up their plants or chasing Hitler the cockerel!

Audrey hurried down the stairs behind me. She'd stopped coming downstairs on her bottom now, but she had to put one foot down first, then bring the other to it; she still wasn't big enough to walk down the stairs properly like normal people.

Maureen and I were going out early bottletop collecting. We'd agreed that one day was enough to collect in our road, then I would ask Grandma to ask her neighbours, and maybe Auntie Maude could get some from Park Grange. That house was always full of people, so they would use up a lot of bottles. Maureen was going to visit her Auntie Beryl for a few days, so she would see how many she could collect there.

"Let's start with our side of the street," said Maureen as she slammed her front door behind her. "We'll start at the bottom and work our way to the top, and finish at Mrs Ennis' house."

I looked at Maureen in surprise. Sometimes she was a lot cleverer than she looked! Mrs Ennis liked children and always had a biscuit tin on her sideboard in case any of the neighbours popped round. If we finished our morning's collecting there, she might even ask us in for a glass of milk and a biscuit!

We made our way down the street, knocking at each door. I kept looking around over my shoulders to see if anyone else from our school had decided to start in our road, but they'd all either gone to another road or they were still sleeping. Lazy lot! All the more chance for us of winning that certificate.

At some houses there was no answer because people were at work or out shopping, but by the time we got to Mrs Ennis' house we had doubled our collection of bottletops.

Maureen rattled the knocker on Mrs Ennis' door. We could hear bolts being drawn back and looked at each other worriedly. Mrs Ennis was old; maybe we shouldn't have knocked there so early; maybe we'd woken her.

The door opened and Mrs Ennis' cat, Smudge, poked his head through the gap. Maureen knelt down to stroke him.

"Good morning, Mrs Ennis," I said, relieved to see that she was dressed and already in her apron. There was a wonderful smell coming from the kitchen; she must have been baking already.

"Hello girls," she replied, "what can I do for you two?"

I explained our task, while Maureen carried on playing with the cat. If we won the certificate it wouldn't be through any efforts of hers, I thought, feeling annoyed.

"I think I can find a couple of bottletops for you," said Mrs Ennis, opening the door wider. "Why don't you come in while I have a look."

We followed her in, wiping our feet carefully on the mat, and perched on the edge of her settee.

The house was spotless, and she had so many ornaments and knick knacks!

"I've just made some oat flapjacks," Mrs Ennis called from the kitchen, to the accompanying sound of drawers being opened and shut. "I used honey instead of butter and sugar, but I think they'll taste good. Would you girls like one each with a glass of milk?"

Maureen and I looked at each other and grinned.

"Yes, please, Mrs Ennis!" we chorused.

Our milk and flapjacks arrived on a tray, laid with a lace-edged napkin, the milk in pretty glasses with gold rims, and flowers painted on the sides, just as if we were real grown-up visitors.

Mrs Ennis shuffled into the kitchen again and returned clutching a paper bag. Six more bottletops!

"Thank you, Mrs Ennis!" we spluttered, through mouthfuls of flapjack.

~*~

Walking back up the road, we met two boys who we recognised from the top class. One of them was swinging a bucket by its handle, and they were talking excitedly.

They stopped when they saw us with our drawstring bag.

"Collecting bottletops?" asked the smaller boy. We nodded.

"How many've you got?"

I did the sum quickly, counting on my fingers. Thirteen from the alley, another twelve from the first houses, then Mrs Ennis' six. . . .

"Thirty-one!" I said, proudly.

The bigger boy swung the bucket up so we could look into

it and gave it a shake to rattle the bottletops. There were loads! At least fifty!

I looked at Maureen and our faces fell.

The boys laughed. "Keep collecting," said the bigger boy. "You're not doing too bad, but we're going to win that certificate!"

~*~

We walked back up the street slowly, dragging our feet. Where could we get enough to make sure that we won?

Then I remembered what Mum had said at tea time.

"Let's go and see old Mr Bryant!" I said, grabbing Maureen's wrist.

"Oh, no!" She shrank back. "He's scary! My mum won't let me talk to him."

"You don't have to talk to him," I said, "I'll do the talking! Come on!"

She still hung back.

"What's the matter? Are you scared of an old man?"

"Yes!" she whimpered. I was worried she was going to cry.

"I know!" I said, "Let's go to my house and get Scamp. No-one will hurt us if we've got a dog with us."

I knew that the only way Scamp would protect us from anyone would be to lick them to death, but it made Maureen feel better, so we ran back to collect the dog, and walked down the other side of the street to knock at Mr Bryant's door.

The door opened and a strange smell wafted out. It was quite strong, and for a minute I couldn't speak.

Mr Bryant stood on the mat and looked at us with his watery red eyes, glaring out from under bushy eyebrows.

He was wearing torn trousers with braces over one of those grey, long-sleeved vests I'd seen on the washing line, and his slippers were covered in ash and dust.

"H . . . hello, Mr Bryant," I said nervously, as he swayed in the doorway.

"What do you want?" he asked, but it sounded more like "warrayouwan?"

"We're collecting bottletops for school," I explained, holding up the bag for him to see and giving it a little shake. "My Mum said you would probably have a few."

He glared hard at me. "Oh, she did, did she?" He sounded angry. I nodded, feebly. Had I said something wrong?

He leaned down and looked at me more closely.

"You're Amy Ford's girl, aren't you?" I nodded again.

"She's a good girl, Amy," he slurred, leaning against the door post. "When my Florrie had dif . . . diphtheria, Amy Ford was the only woman in this street who came to help me. She couldn't help Florrie, it was too late, but none of these other women helped, they all kept their nets closed and ignored us. She's a good girl, your mum," he repeated.

His eyes looked very far away, as though he was going to cry. Not another one! It was bad enough Maureen being a cry-baby, but I didn't want to see a grown-up cry.

"So, have you got any bottletops we can have, please, Mr Bryant?" I asked, reminding him of why we'd come.

His eyes re-focussed on me. "Come through, I've got some in the shed. Bring the dog, he'll be fine in here."

Maureen tugged on the back of my cardigan, but I shook her off and grabbed her wrist firmly, pulling her with me.

The house was a complete contrast to Mrs Ennis'; everything was covered in dust, there was cigarette ash on the carpet, and piles of dirty plates in the sink.

Mr Bryant led us through to the back door and out the back of the house.

The garden surprised us both. The grass was long, and needed cutting, and there were the old grey vests and pants on the line, but on the concrete outside the door was a pair of old-fashioned wooden chairs with pretty cushions, the kind of chairs you can sit in with your feet up and lean right back, and beside one of the chairs was a small round metal table with a beautiful multi-coloured top that shone in the sun.

Mr Bryant opened the shed door and rummaged inside, clattering around among tools and pots of paint, and emerged with cobwebs in his hair and a small sack in his hand.

He knelt down on the concrete, clinging to the back of one of the chairs to steady himself, and tipped the contents of the sack out on to the floor. bottletops! There must have been at least two hundred!

Mr Bryant heaved himself back to his feet and looked at us.

"You see that table?" he asked, waving his hand at it. "Have a closer look at it."

We stepped closer and examined the table. The whole of the top of it was covered in bottletops, arranged in a circular pattern, so that the different colours spiralled out from the centre. They were set into something hard, and had been coated with varnish to make a smooth, shiny table top.

"I made that when my Florrie was alive," he said, softly, his voice sounding more even.

"We used to sit out here on those old steamer chairs; I found those at the dump and did them up, and she made the cushions. Every evening in the summer we used to sit out here after tea and I'd have a bottle of beer, and she'd have a milk stout. I saved all those lids and set them into the table top. I was saving more tops to make a pair to it when she died . . . I don't feel like doing it now, so you girls might as well take them for your battleship."

I stood looking from the table to his face, to the bottletops and back again, feeling like *I* wanted to cry now!

Maureen surprised me by running to Mr Bryant and giving him a big hug! She still hadn't spoken to him, though.

I hugged him too, and thanked him, and Maureen and I scooped up all the bottletops and put them back into the sack.

"Goodbye, Mr Bryant, and thank you." I hugged him again

as we left. We lugged the sack across the street and round through the alley.

"Bottletops for battleships!" shouted Maureen.

"Bottletops for battleships!" I repeated.

"Battletops for bottleships! Bottle taps for battle sheep! Shipple tabs for topple bots!" We crashed into the lean-to, laughing ourselves silly, with tears pouring down our faces.

~*~

Over tea, I told Mum and Daddy about our day. Daddy looked up sharply at Mum when I said we'd visited Mr Bryant, but when I repeated what he'd said about Mummy visiting his wife when she was ill, Daddy reached out and took Mummy's hand and gave it a squeeze.

"I didn't know about that, Ducks," he said softly, and kissed her on the forehead.

Mum smiled and squeezed his hand back. "I told you old Sid was harmless," she said.

~*~

When school opened on the following Monday, there was a lot of excitement. Individual children, pairs, and groups lugged sacks, boxes and buckets to the caretaker's room, where they were labelled with the names of the children who had collected them, and locked up for safety, to be counted. We would find out at the special assembly tomorrow who would be presented with the certificate. At lunchtime, the two boys from the top class tracked us down.

"So, did you get any more after we saw you?" the bigger boy asked.

"Oh yes!" Maureen started, but I stamped on her foot. "Ow!" She elbowed me in the ribs but I ignored her.

"Yes, we got a few more from our aunties and grandmas," I said, casually, and they walked off grinning.

"What did you stamp on my foot for?!" Maureen shouted indignantly.

"We don't want everyone to know how many we got!" I hissed at her. She sulked the rest of the afternoon and refused to talk to me.

~*~

"Good morning, children," said Miss Manning, smiling. "I really think that this is the quietest and most attentive that I have ever seen you! You all want to know who collected the most bottletops, don't you?"

"Yes, Miss!" we all answered enthusiastically.

"I have the list of the top three here," she continued. "In third place, Denis Pegram from Class One, who collected one hundred and thirteen bottletops." We all clapped. I knew that Denis' grandad ran a pub, so that wasn't a surprise.

"In second place. . . ." Miss Manning paused. "Stuart Clark and Billy Hammond from Class Three, who collected two hundred and seven." The two boys with the bucket.

Maureen craned her neck round to stare at them as the applause rang out, and I nudged her, hard.

"And the winner . . . s . . . are. . . ." The whole school was holding its breath.

"Maureen Fielding and Sylvia Ford from Class Two, who collected an incredible two hundred and seventy three! Come up and collect your certificates, girls."

The whole school clapped as Maureen and I stood up and walked out in front of the assembly. And it wasn't just one certificate, we got one each! They were beautiful, with the flags of the commonwealth all around the edges, signed by Miss Manning, and with our names written in ink in her lovely copperplate writing.

~*~

Back in our classroom, the rest of the class gathered round to look at our certificates, and everyone wanted to hold them, so that eventually Miss Hills took them away and put them in her desk for safety, until the end of school.

On the way home, Billy and Stuart caught up with us. "Well done, you two," said Billy. "I'd like to know how you managed to find so many!"

I looked at Maureen. "A friend helped us," she said.

~*~

"I've got a frame we can put your certificate in," said Mum, her voice muffled as she rummaged in the cupboard under the stairs.

She emerged with a dark wood frame in her hand, and laid it on the table to take the back off.

As I watched her fit the certificate inside and close the swivel clasps over the velvet frame back I noticed that she had cobwebs in her hair, and it reminded me of something.

"Mum? Mr Bryant's house is a real mess. It doesn't look like he knows how to dust or clean or anything. Could we go over there and help him one Saturday? He was so kind, giving us all those bottletops, and I think he's lonely."

Mum took the nail she was holding from between her lips and tapped it into the wall with three quick strokes of the hammer.

She laid down the hammer and ruffled my hair.

"Yes, we'll do that, Sylvie. What a good idea. You're a good girl."

She pulled one of the dining chairs across to the wall and helped me onto it so I could hang my certificate myself. Daddy came in from the kitchen for the grand certificate hanging ceremony. I felt like the Queen, launching a ship!

"I'm very proud of you, Sylvie," said Mum.

Audrey clapped her hands. "Sylvie's won a cerstitificup!" she shouted, and Mum laughed and swung her up for a cuddle.

Chapter Eleven

The Big House

"Maude! What are you doing home at this time of the morning?" asked Mum.

We were all surprised to see Auntie Maude open Grandma's front door, and she seemed to be enjoying the looks on our faces.

"The Whitefields have gone to their cottage in Sussex for six weeks," she explained, "so we're all on light duties, just keeping the place ticking over while they're away. Dusting and that. I'm going up there today to sheet up the furniture and polish the floor in the big hall, and I thought the girls could come with me, have a look around, and maybe help a bit." She winked at me, and hoisted Audrey on to her hip.

"If you're sure they won't be in the way...?" Mum looked anxious. "I don't want you getting in trouble with your employers."

"They'll be fine," Auntie Maude reassured her. "I'll find them plenty to do to keep them out of trouble."

~*~

The long drive up to Park Grange House was made of tiny stones that slithered and scrunched underfoot. The house looked enormous from the gate, and it just kept getting bigger and bigger as we walked closer. I was quite glad that the Whitefield family were away; I wouldn't know what to say to anyone who lived in such a grand house.

The big double front doors had beautiful coloured glass panels in them, and I imagined how it would look inside with the light shining through and making rainbows, but Auntie

Maude kept on walking, round the side of the house, and through a door at the back, next to a glass house that stood at the top of a sweeping walled garden.

"Wipe your feet, girls," Auntie instructed as we opened the door to a warm, sparkling clean kitchen. There were white tiles as far as you could see, and standing at a scrubbed table was a tall, well-built lady in a white overall who was scouring a pan from a pile set beside her elbow.

"Good morning, Cook," said Auntie, hanging her hat on a peg beside the door. "These are my nieces, Sylvia and Audrey. They've come to spend the day and help a bit. I'm going to get that hall floor polished today, so they can help with that."

I didn't like the sound of that, it sounded like hard work!

"There's plenty of milk in the fridge, girls, if you'd like a drink before you start work," said Cook. She turned to Auntie Maude and whispered, "Shocking waste, the food they've left in the fridge! And a war on and everything. Mrs W said to share out all the perishables among the staff, so have a look and see if there's anything you and your mum want before you go."

Auntie Maude nodded, and patted the large shopping bag she'd brought with her. She tucked the bag down beside the door and poured glasses of milk for Audrey and me. The fridge was enormous! We kept our milk in the scullery at home, in a bucket of cold water if it was a really hot day.

"Come on then, you two," said Auntie, as Audrey finally drained her glass. Audrey had a milk moustache, but I could tell she didn't care.

Auntie led us out of the kitchen into a long passage with a door at the end. It looked like a perfectly normal door, but when she opened it there was the biggest room I had ever seen!

"This is the hall, where the family have all their dinner parties and dances," said Auntie. "There's usually a big table right down the middle of the room, but it's been moved so we can get this floor polished. You two stay here a minute, and don't touch anything!"

Auntie Maude disappeared back through the door into the passage, and we heard her rattling around in a cupboard. She emerged carrying a bucket with some bottles of cleaning things in it, some cloths, and what looked like a broom, but no broom we'd ever seen before. It had a wide head, about four feet long and over a foot wide, and instead of bristles it had a flat head, made of what looked like strips of rag.

Auntie ducked back into the passage, and came out again with two pairs of ugly looking sandals that looked much too big for any normal feet. They had cloths tied over the soles.

Auntie Maude dumped everything in a pile, and straightened up to smile at us, puffing a bit.

"Now, then!" she said. "You two stand against that back wall for a few minutes, then we'll get started."

She took one of the bottles from the bucket and walked across the room to the opposite end from us, then, walking backwards, she dribbled sticky looking liquid across the floor, zig zagging from one side of the room to the other.

When she finally arrived back at our end of the room, she crouched down and strapped a pair of the ugly sandals on over her shoes, then sat me on one knee while she crouched, and strapped the other pair to my feet.

Finally, she said to Audrey, "Come here, Chick, sit yourself down on this broom and we'll go for a ride, shall we?"

Audrey sat down cross-legged on the wide broom, looking up at Auntie as though she thought our aunt had lost her mind!

"Ready?" said Auntie. We nodded, although we weren't sure what we were ready for!

Auntie started to push the wide broom head across the floor, smearing the polish that she had spread on the floor as she went.

Audrey squealed as the broom started to move, then laughed delightedly as she glided across the room.

"Come on, Sylvie," called Auntie Maude, "skate!"

I watched her feet; she was sliding one foot forward across the floor, then the other, without lifting them. I copied what she was doing, and found myself gliding across the floor behind her. This was fun!

We glided all over that huge wooden floor, up and down, up and down, until all the polish was worked into the wood, then Auntie wrapped a cloth around the head of the broom, changed the cloths on our "sandals" for new ones, and off we went again, bringing the floor up to a lovely shine.

By the time we had finished, we were all breathless from laughing and skating, and ravenously hungry.

Auntie packed the cleaning things back into the passage cupboard and we ran back to the kitchen to see what Cook could find us for lunch.

"So, did you enjoy polishing the floor, kids?" asked Cook.

Audrey nodded, scattering bits of spam from the sandwich she was munching.

"That was the most fun work I've ever done!" I told Cook, and she laughed.

"Some houses have big electrical polishers now, but they're heavy to move around, and your auntie prefers to do it the old way."

"What can we clean this afternoon?" I asked, eagerly.

"I need to put dust sheets on all the furniture in the bedrooms this afternoon," said Auntie Maude. "I'll keep Audrey with me; there are some picture books in the nursery that she can look at, and you can explore anywhere on the top floor, Sylvie, but promise me you won't *touch anything!* Mrs Whitefield'll have my guts for garters if anything gets broken!"

"Take them up the front stairs, Maude," said Cook. "They can pretend they're princesses going to a ball." She winked at us and wiped bits of food off Audrey's face with a cloth.

Auntie led us through another passage, and through another door, which came out under a staircase, or actually half a staircase!

We were in the front hall, the other side of the double doors with the beautiful coloured glass. The floor was made of black and white tiles, like a draughts board, and where the light shone through the glass the white tiles were coloured red, green, blue, yellow. . . all the colours of the rainbow.

The stairs led up from both sides of the hallway, and curved in to meet at the top where a wider staircase carried on upwards to a long landing.

"Come on, Audrey!" I cried, "I bet I can beat you to the top!"

I walked slowly up one side of the stairs, to give her a chance, while she stumped up the other side, and just as we got to the top I pretended to have a stitch, to let her win.

"I won! I won! I'm a pincess!" shouted Audrey.

"Well then, your highness," Auntie Maude said, dropping a low curtsey to Audrey, "let's find you a book to look at while I get on with sheeting these rooms. Sylvie, off you go and explore, and remember; don't touch anything, and stay on this floor!"

I walked slowly down the landing, at first not daring to do more than peep into the bedrooms, but after a while I became bolder and ventured in. It didn't look as though any of the rooms had been used for a long time; there were no personal things lying around anywhere. Maybe these rooms were just for visitors, and the family used other bedrooms.

All along the landing were pictures. Some were photographs, and some were paintings of people in old-fashioned dresses and suits.

My favourite picture was of a little girl in white frilly dress and high button boots, who had her arms wrapped around the neck of a big golden dog. The dog and the little girl's hair were almost exactly the same colour. I stood and stared at that painting for a long while, wondering who the girl was, and what happened to her.

I could hear Auntie Maude talking to Audrey as they moved from room to room, Auntie smoothing clean white dust sheets over the furniture, and Audrey babbling about the pictures in the book she had borrowed.

I wandered to the end of the landing, and around a tight bend. There was a staircase, hidden behind the grandly papered walls. The walls of the staircase weren't grand at all, they were just plain distemper, and the carpet on the stairs was plain brown.

I started to walk up, then remembered what Auntie had said about staying on the same floor. I hesitated, then kept on climbing. The stairs were on the same floor, weren't they?

The staircase turned another corner, and there was no carpet at all on this part. Right at the top was a plain wooden door with a big brass handle with a thumb latch.

I put my hand out and gripped the handle. I listened. Silence. Auntie hadn't noticed that I was missing.

I pressed my thumb on the latch and pushed the door. It was locked. Disappointed, I let go of the latch and it flipped back up with a big clatter.

"Who? Whoooo? Whoooooooooooo?" said a voice from behind the door.

I screamed and hurled myself down the stairs, two at a time, jumping the last four in one leap.

Auntie came running from one of the bedrooms.

"Sylvie! Whatever's the matter? Are you hurt?"

She kneeled down in front of me and gathered me into her arms. I was sobbing in fear by now, and buried my face in her shoulder.

"This house is h . . . haunted!" I wailed.

"Sylvie, darling, what are you talking about?" Auntie Maude rocked me and stroked my hair until I calmed down enough to tell her the story.

"I went up the stairs at the end," I pointed back over my shoulder. "I know you said not to, but I . . . I . . . forgot. I tried to open the door but it was locked, and this voice in the room said "Who? Whoooooo?" It was a ghoooooooost!" I started sobbing again.

Auntie held me tight, and I could feel her shaking. So it was a ghost! She was just as scared as I was.

She pushed me away from her a little and lifted my chin with her finger to make me look into her eyes. She was laughing!

Tears were streaming down her face, and she was shaking with giggles.

"Oh, Sweetie, there's no ghost! That's just an owl! The owls got in through a loose tile in the roof and made a nest there. They'll be having baby owls soon, so Mr Whitehead locked that door so they can bring the babies up in peace. You know owls sleep during the day and fly at night?"

I nodded, sniffing. "They're nocturnal," I said, "We did it at school last term."

"Clever girl to remember," said Auntie. "You see, you woke them up and they were a bit startled, so they called out. They were probably more scared than you."

I doubted that, but it was nice to know it was just birds and not a ghost!

Audrey came toddling along the landing, holding out the picture book, open at a picture of a lady in a long red dress.

"Who?" asked Audrey, pointing at the picture. "Who?"

Auntie and I looked at each other and burst out laughing.

Chapter Twelve

Oh I Do Like To Be Beside The Seaside

"Come in, Amy, and have a cup of tea while we sort out what's happening tomorrow," said Auntie Maude when Mum arrived to collect us from Grandma's.

I pricked up my ears; what was happening tomorrow?

Mum kissed Audrey and me and followed Auntie Maude through to the kitchen.

"I'll get down to your house at about half past seven," I head Auntie say. "There's a train at eight; that'll give us time to get to the station. Don't worry about food, we'll get some chips when we get there."

We? Chips when we get there? Who was going where? And by train! And chips!

"What's happening tomorrow, Mum?" I asked as we settled ourselves on the back seat of the bus to go home.

"You'll find out soon enough," she replied mysteriously.

~*~

Daddy hadn't yet left for work when there came a knock at the door next morning. I ran to open it and there was Auntie Maude, with a big bulging straw bag hung on her shoulder.

"Are we ready?" she asked.

"Yes, but where are we *going*?" I shouted impatiently.

"The seaside!" said Auntie with a big grin.

"Seaside, seaside!" yelled Audrey, hopping around on one foot, which she had just learned to do.

I bent down to ask her, "Do you know what the seaside is, Aud?"

"Seaside, seaside!" she yelled again, laughing. She hadn't got a clue, really!

We kissed Mum and Daddy goodbye, and set off with Auntie to walk the twenty minutes to the station at the other side of the village.

I had been on a train before, when we went to the pantomime in London before the war, but Audrey hadn't, so she was very quiet when we arrived at the station and Auntie bought our tickets from the lady behind the glass.

All around the ticket office were posters asking, "Is Your Journey Really Necessary?" and as we walked to the platform to wait for our train I pulled Auntie's sleeve and asked in a whisper, "Is our journey really necessary, Auntie Maude?"

"Yes!" she said firmly. "And if anyone asks why we're travelling, you two just keep quiet and let me do the talking." She winked.

The train arrived with a big rattle and clatter and a hiss of steam, and Audrey hid behind Auntie Maude, whimpering a bit, but once we were on the train and settled in the seats, she started to get excited, and when the doors slammed and the train started to move, she squealed loudly. There were some other people in the carriage, and they smiled at her, despite the noise she was making.

The train picked up speed, and we flashed through a couple of stations, but there were no signs on the platforms to say which stations they were; the signs had all been taken away so that if the Germans invaded they wouldn't know where they were. That didn't really make sense to me; they'd have to ask for a ticket, so surely they'd know where they were going!

I nudged Auntie Maude and asked anxiously, "How will we know when we're there?"

"We're going to the end of the line, so don't worry. The train can't go any further, or it'd end up in the sea!"

~*~

The journey took about two and a half hours, but there was so much to look at that we didn't have time to get bored. We passed by farmers' fields where land girls were working with horses. In the distance, we could see barrage balloons hovering in the clear air, and at one point we chugged along beside a canal, where we saw small brick-built huts every now and then. Auntie said they were called pill boxes, and they were for soldiers to hide in and shoot from if the Germans invaded and came sailing up the canal.

An old man in uniform came walking down the aisle of the train towards us, calling, "Tickets, please," and having a short conversation with each person as he stopped and clipped their ticket with what looked like a little pair of pliers.

Auntie held out our tickets and the man peered over his glasses at us, and then looked at the tickets.

"What is the purpose of your journey, madam?" he asked.

"My husband's in the army camp, and he's due to be posted, so I'm taking the girls down to see him before he goes," she lied.

Auntie lied!

I could see Audrey looking confused, and she looked like she was about to speak up, so I grabbed her in a tight hug and buried her face in my chest.

"Don't get upset, Audrey," I said, playing along, "Daddy will be fine." I sniffed a little and looked up at the man with big eyes.

He nodded, cleared his throat, and clipped our tickets.

As he walked away Auntie winked at me, then quickly clapped her hand over Audrey's mouth as she started, "But Aun. . . ."

~*~

Eventually the train pulled into yet another station and stopped in a big cloud of steam. Auntie gathered up her basket and smoothed down Audrey's dress as she slid down from the seat.

"Here we are, Chickens!" She smiled and helped us climb down from the high train step to the platform.

There was no sign of the sea!

Auntie saw the disappointed look on my face and tweaked my pigtail.

"Just a short walk and you'll see the sea," she said, and took a hand of each of us as we set off.

We turned out of the station into a long road with very grand houses on each side. Some of the houses had balconies, and most had names, like "Sea View" or "Beach House". Auntie said that they were hotels where people stayed on holiday, but most were filled with soldiers and evacuees now. But we still couldn't see the sea.

At the end of the road we came to what looked like a high street, but across the road all we could see was a wall with railings on top, and the railings had barbed wire wrapped round them. Beyond that was just sky.

We crossed the road and Auntie Maude lifted us onto a bench that stood near the railings . . . and there was the sea!

The beach below us looked very stony, but Auntie said there was another part of the beach further down through the town where the sand was smooth and we could play. We wouldn't be able to paddle in the sea, though, as there were defences built all along the shore to stop anyone from landing there.

"I'm hungry!" said Audrey. As usual, her stomach was more important than anything, even looking at the sea!

"That's the sea air," laughed Auntie. "Let's go for a stroll on the pier and then we'll get some chips."

We skipped along the promenade singing, "Oh, I do like to be beside the seaside. . . ," so loudly that people turned and smiled at us.

The pier was a big wide road on stilts that went right out into the sea, and it was made of planks of wood, so you could look through the gaps between the planks and see the sea lapping against the metal legs that held it up down below. The legs were wrapped in barbed wire, too.

Audrey was a bit nervous at first, worried that she might fall through the gaps, but she soon got used to it.

We couldn't go right to the end of the pier, as there was a hut on the end, surrounded by sandbags, which Auntie said was a gun emplacement manned by the Local Defence Volunteers, but we had fun running up and down and playing hide and seek behind the booths. Most of them were closed as there was no-one to work in them; there were more important jobs for people to do than work sideshows at the seaside, but there were a few food stalls open, and we followed our noses to one selling fish and chips.

"Three portions of chips and one tea, please, and what fish have you got?" Auntie asked the lady behind the stall. "Any cod?"

"Sorry love, it's Snoek," the lady replied as she dished up the chips into newspaper cones.

"I'll give it a miss then, thanks. Just the chips and tea, please," said Auntie, and dug in her purse for coins.

We scattered our chips with salt and vinegar and sat on a bench to eat them.

The seagulls kept diving down to try to steal our chips, making Audrey scream, so eventually Auntie threw them a chip to make them go away. The chips somehow tasted better at the seaside than when we had them from the chip van at home, and we soon polished them off, even Audrey, whose eyes were usually too big for her belly.

"Come on then, girls, let's walk that lot off!" said Auntie, collecting up the chip wrappers to throw away. "Let's see if we can find you two an ice cream on the way to the sandy beach."

Licking away at our ice creams, we sauntered along the road. Auntie said it was called "the front", which was confusing, because the war was happening at the front, according to the newsreaders on the wireless. Auntie said it was a different kind of front.

Seagulls apparently like ice cream too, as they kept dive bombing us. Ducking to get away from them, Audrey managed to drop her ice cream out of her cone, and started bawling, but Auntie Maude gave Audrey her own ice cream and she stopped crying.

As we walked through the town, we came to the end of the part where the houses were and passed what looked like a small village of one-storey houses behind a high fence. More barbed wire.

Auntie told us that before the war it had been a holiday camp, but it had been turned into a training camp where men went to learn how to be soldiers and fight, before they were sent off to the war.

It didn't look very holiday-ish now.

There were two enormous brick towers along the front, facing out over the sea. Auntie said that they had been built over a hundred years earlier, when we were fighting the French, so that soldiers could keep a watch over the sea, and now they were being used again, except this time we were friends with the French.

"Why do we have to keep having wars, Auntie Maude?" I asked.

"I don't know, Sylvie love, and if we ever work that one out, maybe the world'll be a better place. Now, look over here, this is the way onto the beach."

There was an area where the wall was low enough to sit on and swing over onto the beach. Audrey needed a bit of a leg-up, but she jumped down easily enough the other side.

The sand was lovely and smooth. Auntie rummaged in her big straw bag and pulled out a thin rug, but the bag was still bulging. She had our gas masks in there, but they didn't take up that much room! We sat on the rug and Auntie dipped into the bag again.

"I brought your Uncle Johnny's old bucket and spade. Let's see how big a sandcastle we can build before we have to go home!"

Building the sandcastle was so much fun! It had a big round base, then we used the bucket to mould turrets, which we decorated with shells, then we dug a big moat all around it.

We couldn't fill the moat with sea water, because the sea was too far out, but it looked wonderful!

We sat on the rug admiring our castle, and Auntie brought out a packet of mints to suck on as we watched the waves and listened to the seagulls. Auntie sat with her back to the low wall and had what she called "forty winks". Audrey was nodding off, too, and I may have had a little doze myself, as the next thing I remember is Auntie exclaiming, "Goodness, girls! We need to get to the station; it's half past three, and the train is at ten past four. We'll have to get a move on!"

She gathered up the bag and its contents, and we hopped back over the wall and started marching up the road to the station. Audrey just couldn't walk fast enough, so Auntie slung the straw bag across my chest so it bumped on my hip as I walked, and hoisted Audrey onto her shoulders.

We made it to the station with ten minutes to spare, and Auntie Maude bought a bottle of lemonade for us to share on the way home.

We settled into the carriage, which was so full that Audrey had to sit on Auntie Maude's lap, and before we'd passed two stations on the way home, we were all asleep.

Some instinct woke Auntie just before we reached our station, luckily, or we might have ended up in London!

We wearily trudged up the hill to the high street, and around the corner to our road. It felt like we had been away for weeks, on a real holiday, not just a day out. I was quite surprised to see the street looking just the same as it had that morning.

We clattered in as Mum opened the front door, showering grains of sand on the door mat. Mum swung Audrey up for a cuddle.

"Oh, my tired baby! Did Auntie Maude wear you out?" she laughed. "Why are you rattling, Chickie?"

Mum sat Audrey on her hip and watched in surprise as Audrey's hand went into her pocket and her podgy little fist pulled out a handful of shells!

"For you," said Audrey, handing them to Mum, then her head drooped, and she fell asleep on Mummy's shoulder.

"It looks like you girls had a good day," said Mum, smoothing my sea-breeze ruffled hair where it had come loose from its pigtail.

"Oh, it was a super day! The best day ever!"

Part Four
1942

Chapter Thirteen

The Runaway

I pushed my copy of The Beano across the table with a sigh and moved round to another chair to get out of the cold draught from the open front door. Mum had been out there for ages talking to Mrs Samson; I knew she wouldn't invite her in, the dusting and sweeping hadn't been done yet, but even so, it was only the second of January! Brrr!

It was nice to be off school, and even nicer that Mum had been given time off work over Christmas so Audrey and I could stay at home all the school holidays, but it was cold and dull; Maureen was at her auntie's again, and I had run out of anything to do.

The voices murmured on and on at the front door, and I couldn't concentrate on my comic.

I crept into the front room, not really to listen to what they were talking about, just to see if they were anywhere near finishing.

Audrey was sitting on the floor with crayons and a colouring book, but she wasn't colouring, she was cuddling Scamp and plaiting his tail, which he didn't look too happy about.

I held my finger to my lips to tell her to be quiet and tiptoed nearer to the hall door.

"So how long do you have to have bed rest?" I heard Mum say.

"A week in bed when I come home, at least, but then I'm not allowed to lift anything or do any exercise, so of course I can't walk far, which is why I wondered if your Sylvie would help out."

I strained my ears to hear how Mrs Samson wanted me to help, but they had changed the subject and were talking about one of those things that ladies whisper about. I knew it had to be either stocking tops or the District Nurse; whenever Mum talked about either, she made the words with her mouth but no sound came out.

I knew stocking tops were rude; they were one of those things you weren't supposed to show, like knickers, but I felt sorry for the District Nurse that people whispered about her. Nurse Betty wasn't rude!

I heard my name mentioned again. "I'll speak to Sylvie, but I'm sure she'll love it. Maybe she could start this afternoon, to get to know them?"

"Good idea, send her round after dinner and I'll introduce her to them."

Introduce me to who?

Mrs Samson said her goodbyes and I scuttled back to the kitchen, to look busy reading my comic when Mum came in.

"Goodness, it's chilly in here! Are you warm enough, girls?" asked Mum, setting the kettle on the stove.

"Yes, Mum," I answered, "I am now. Mum? What did Mrs Samson want?"

"She wants you to do a little job for her, Sylvie," said Mum, sitting down to wait for the kettle to boil. "She's going into hospital next week for an operation and when she comes home she's not allowed to do very much." I was right, it was the District Nurse they'd been talking about.

"So," Mum continued, "she wondered if you would like to walk her dogs for her. She said you can go round after dinner and meet them, and I'd like you to pop down to the library and change my books for me, so you can kill two birds with one stone and walk the dogs at the same time. Better not take Scamp this first time; he doesn't know them, and he might play up. It's easier to manage two dogs than three."

"What kind of dogs are they? Are they big?"

Mum laughed. "No, they're dachshunds; sausage dogs, you know, the long low ones with short legs and long ears."

"What are their names?" I asked. I was looking forward to meeting these dogs.

"I don't know, you'll find out when you go round there after dinner. Now, how about opening that tin of spam for me while I put the potatoes on?"

~*~

Mum handed me a string bag containing the two books that she wanted to take back to the library.

"Ask Miss Jeffreys for something similar; she knows which ones I've read already, and remember, no Ethel M. Dell, no Ruby M. Ayres and no 'I' books." Mum didn't like books where the people in the stories were the ones telling the story. She said she couldn't imagine how they could possibly know what the other people in the books were thinking.

I wrapped up warm in my new red pixie hood that Mum had knitted for me for Christmas. The wide strips of knitted wool tied under my chin, and dangled down over my coat past my waist, and right at the end of each was a pocket, so I could put my hands in there to keep warm and not worry about losing mittens.

I felt very important as I walked down the road to do my errands.

~*~

Mrs Sampson opened her front door and invited me in. There was loud yapping coming from behind the closed kitchen door; the dogs sounded just as excited to meet me as I was to meet them.

"Take your coat off for a bit while you get to know the dogs, or you won't feel the benefit when you go back out," said Mrs Samson, "and I'll bring them out and show you how to fasten their harnesses."

She opened the kitchen door and two small brown dogs came running out, barking excitedly and jumping around in circles.

"This is Fritz," said Mrs Samson, picking up the bigger of the two dogs, "and that's his sister Lolita."

Fancy names for little dogs, I thought, but I wasn't surprised; Mrs Samson's grown up daughter had a fancy name too, she was called Delphine, and she worked as a mannequin in one of the London department stores, dressing up in expensive clothes and walking up and down to show the clothes off to rich ladies who might buy them.

I knelt on the floor to play with the dogs. They were very lively and friendly, climbing on my lap and butting my chin with their heads, and licking my hands, their little tails wagging non-stop.

Mrs Samson took down two small harnesses from the hall rack and held them out to show me how the buckles and straps fastened.

"The blue one is Fritz's and the red one is Lolita's," she said. "I don't use collars on them because their necks are quite thick and their heads are small, so they can slip out of a collar easily."

She showed me how to lift Lolita's front paws and make her step into the front of the harnesses, which she did very eagerly, then I buckled one strap across the back of her neck and the other under her tummy. Those two straps were joined by another one which ran down Lolita's back, and had a ring attached to it. The ring was where her lead clipped on.

Fritz was next, but he wasn't so eager to be put into his harness, and wriggled away a few times before I managed to fasten it tightly.

Once the dogs realised that they were going for a walk, they started to bark and jump around on the door mat.

I bundled myself back into my coat and hood, slung the string bag on my shoulder and took a lead in each hand.

"Ready, dogs?" I asked them. They looked up at me and yapped as though they knew what I was saying.

"Down to the library and back will be a long enough walk for them," said Mrs Samson. "They've only got short legs!" And off we went.

~*~

The dogs marched ahead of me smartly, not looking left or right, and pulling at the leads. I was glad I hadn't brought Scamp along; he wasn't as easy to walk as these two. He would jump around, sometimes hanging back, sometimes trying to pull forward, and stopping to sniff everything on the way. Walking him was more fun, though; these two dogs were nice, but a bit boring to walk. Maybe I just didn't know them well enough yet.

I looped their leads onto the hook attached to the wall of the library, beside the bicycle rack, and twisted the loops round the hook a few times to make sure they couldn't pull them off and run away.

The library was warm and quiet. A few elderly men were sitting in the reading room with newspapers on their laps and pipes in their mouths, and the air in there was full of blue smoke.

Miss Jeffreys peered over her glasses at me as I slid the books out of the bag and onto the high counter. She was very stern, and always telling people to be quiet. I don't think she liked children very much, either.

"Mummy said can she change these for something similar, please, but no Ethel M. Dell, no Ruby M. Ayres and no 'I' books."

Miss Jeffreys sniffed and took the books. "Mrs Ford?" she asked. I nodded.

Miss Jeffreys took a little wooden box labelled with an F from under the counter and flipped through to find the two little card envelopes with Mummy's name on them. She took them out, plucked out the white card slips from them, stamped the slips with the date, and slid them back into the books.

She kept the tickets behind the counter and called to the assistant librarian.

"Miss Brown? Please man the counter while I go to the romance section."

Miss Brown stepped behind the counter and smiled at me. She was young and fun. Our class had been taken to the library for story time one afternoon last term and Miss Brown had read a really exciting adventure story to us. Miss Jeffreys didn't like people reading out loud in her quiet library, and had been very sniffy about it, but Miss Brown didn't care.

"Are you enjoying the school holidays?" she asked in a whisper.

"Yes," I whispered back, "but I'm looking forward to going back to school. I'm walking a neighbour's dogs for her today. I hope they're behaving themselves outside!"

Miss Brown laughed, causing a loud "SHHHHH!" to come from the romance aisle where Miss Jeffreys had just finished selecting Mum's books.

"You may go back to your duties, Miss Brown," she said as she glided back behind the counter. Funny how it never seemed to matter that Miss Jeffreys talked at the top of her voice.

I walked round to the "out" counter and waited for the part of visiting the library that I liked best.

Miss Jeffreys flipped open the cover of the first book, slid out the little white card from its pocket, and picked up the date stamp.

Crash, bang, crash, bang, went the stamp. First on the ink pad, then on the card, then back to the ink pad, and finally onto the inside page of the book itself.

The card was slipped into one of Mum's tickets, and back into the F box.

Another set of crashing and banging, and the books were handed over.

"Thank you, Miss Jeffreys, goodbye!" I said loudly, and ran out of the library before she could tell me to "shhhhhh".

~*~

As I opened the door, Fritz and Lolita were jumping excitedly, pulling at their leads. I swung my bag onto my shoulder and bent to unwind the leads from the hook, but Fritz was too impatient. He must have been holding his breath to make himself bigger when I put the harness on, or something. Mrs Samson had checked the buckles and they were tight, but now with a sudden jerk Fritz managed to slip completely out of his harness, and off he ran down the road!

"Fritz!" I yelled, "come back here!" but he just kept running.

I snatched up the empty harness and lead, slipped the loop of Lolita's lead over my wrist, and hared off after the runaway.

Lolita's little legs twinkled away under her low-slung body, but she just couldn't run fast enough to keep up, and Fritz was disappearing into the distance, so I gathered her up and tucked her under my arm, the book bag banging on my back as I ran.

"Fritz! Fritz! Somebody stop him!" I yelled as I ran down the high street. People were stopping and turning to watch; why didn't they help? I'd only been dog walking one day and I'd managed to lose one of the dogs! What was I going to say to Mrs Samson when I got home with only one dog?

"Fritz! Stop!" I shouted again. A boy was swinging on the park gate and gazed at me open-mouthed as I pounded past yelling "Fritz! Fritz!"

"Have the Germans invaded?" he asked, jumping down and running along after me. "Let's find a policeman!"

"Not the Germans," I panted, "I've lost a dog! I'm going to be in so much trouble." The boy lost interest and dropped behind.

A bus pulled up at the stop ahead and a group of ladies with shopping bags climbed down. I could see Fritz running through them, trying to weave between all the legs and bags. It slowed him down enough that I caught up a bit, but he was still running.

"Come back here you stupid dog!" I screamed, tears pouring down my face, and my throat sore from yelling.

An older boy in a striped apron stepped out of the butcher's shop further down the road to see what the commotion was and immediately realised what was happening. He whipped back into the shop and came running out again with a piece of meat in his hand. He stood in the middle of the pavement and made himself as wide as possible, crouching low with the meat in one hand.

"Here boy, good dog," he called to Fritz, waving the meat as the little dog galloped towards him.

I slowed to a trot; I had a stitch and needed to breathe. Lolita was wriggling under my arm and seemed to be getting heavier with every step.

I thought Fritz was going to run straight past the butcher's boy, but greed got the better of him. He slowed, stopped, sniffed at the meat, and the boy grabbed him!

I panted to a stop, my face wet with tears and my nose running, and bent to hug the naughty dog.

"Oh Fritz!" I sobbed, "I thought I'd lost you!"

"Let me help you strap him in," said the butcher's boy, "and we'll do that harness up good and tight this time!"

I held Fritz firmly while the boy fastened the buckles and gave them a good tug to check that they were tight.

Fritz whimpered slightly, but the boy was stern with him and he knew he was in disgrace.

We straightened up and I gripped both dogs' leads firmly.

"Thank you very much," I said to the boy. "I would never have caught him! That was so clever of you to think of getting the meat!"

"I'm glad we managed to catch him," he said, handing me

a handkerchief from his pocket. "You're a fast runner, but not fast enough to keep up with this little tyke!"

I mopped my face and got my breath back.

"This hanky's all wet now," I said, holding it out. "Do you want it back?"

"No, you keep it," he laughed. "What's your name?"

"Sylvie," I replied. "What's yours?"

"I'm William," he said, "commonly known as Billy." He grinned and held out his hand. I shook it firmly and grinned back at him.

The butcher was standing in the doorway with his arms folding, smiling at us.

"Come on, Billy, if you've finished rescuing damsels in distress for one day, there's work for you to do. Are you all right now?" he asked me.

"Yes, thank you, thanks to Billy!"

They waved as we walked away. Fritz kept turning his head to look up at me as though he knew he had been naughty and had better not try any more tricks.

"How did you get on?" asked Mrs Samson, "Did they behave themselves?"

I looked down at the two dogs. I didn't want to lie to Mrs Samson, but if I told her that Fritz had run away she might not let me walk them again, and I had grown to like them a lot, in spite of how naughty Fritz was.

"We had a really fast walk," I said. "I think they've had plenty of exercise for one day!"

Over tea at home, I told Mum and Daddy the whole story.

When I got to the part where I had run down the high street yelling "Fritz!" at the top of my voice, they both started laughing and Audrey and I joined in. Daddy laughed so much that tears ran down his face, and it was quite a while before any of us could speak.

"Oh, Sylvie!" he gasped eventually, "you were so lucky they didn't call the home guard out, thinking you were running away from German invaders! Maybe Mrs Samson should re-name that dog for the duration of the war!"

Chapter Fourteen

Rosehips, Rosehips, All The Way

"Now don't forget," said Miss Williams as we closed our desks and stood to say "good afternoon" at the end of school, "You all need to bring in a big paper bag tomorrow, as we're going to go collecting rosehips. Good afternoon, Class Three."

"Good afternoon, Miss Williams," we replied together. Miss Williams nodded, and we clattered out of the classroom, chattering about where we could get the biggest paper bag possible.

The sun was low over the church tower as we left school and walked home through the park. It was September now, and the air was starting to get that certain smell that comes at the end of summer; a smell of ripe fruit, turning leaves, and smoke from chimneys, as households started to light fires on chilly evenings.

Maureen and I were now in the top infants' class; this time next year, we would be starting at the Big Girls' school. It was really called St James' School, but everyone called it The Big Girls'.

The boys would go to The Whitefield School, which was set up a long time ago by an ancestor of the family at Park Grange, where Auntie Maude worked.

We felt very important to be some of the oldest children at school, and remembered how nervous we had felt that first day when we sat on the steps and watched the bigger children running and shouting. Maureen wouldn't be eight for a while yet, her birthday was in February, but I would be eight in just a few weeks.

"It'll be nice to get out of the classroom tomorrow," said Maureen. "I hope we get out of Arithmetic!" She was bad at sums, and dreaded when we had to do sums quickly in our heads without writing anything down.

"When we get to the Big Girls', we'll have homework to do," I reminded her, and she groaned.

"Let's make the most of this year, then!" She swung her satchel up by its strap so it made a full circle over her head. "I'll see you in the morning."

~*~

As I helped dry the plates after tea, I remembered the paper bag. "Mum? Have we got a big paper bag I can take to school tomorrow, please?"

Mum wiped the sink down and wrung out the dishcloth.

"What do you need that for?" she asked, opening the cupboard and clattering the clean plates onto the pile. I waited until the last plate was stacked; I knew she wouldn't hear me over the noise.

"We're going out to collect rosehips," I explained. "Miss Williams says they're going to be sent to be made into a syrup so that children can get vitamins they need. Now we can't get oranges and lemons, we need to get these vitamins from somewhere else, that's what she said."

"Go and ask your dad for one of the bags he puts up his Dahlia roots in," she said. "I think he's got some in the shed."

~*~

I ran out to the garden. Audrey was skipping on the concrete outside the lean-to, or trying to. Maureen and I had tried to teach her, but she hadn't got the hang of jumping over the rope yet, she just whirled it about and stepped over it when she remembered, when it wasn't tangled around her feet.

I knew where Daddy would be: at the bottom of the garden, by his dahlia patch. I loved the dahlias as much as he did; they were bright and bold, and cheered up the garden. The rest of the small plot had been turned over to vegetables; we were

Digging For Victory, like it said on the posters, but Daddy said, "That Hitler can't stop me having a bit of beauty in my garden," and planted his dahlias.

He was sitting on the upside-down wheelbarrow, smoking his pipe and absent-mindedly throwing a ball down the path for Scamp, who raced after it, barking madly, picked it up, and brought it back to Daddy to be thrown again, his tail wagging like the clappers. Daddy didn't seem to care that the ball was getting soggier and soggier, as he puffed the smoke from his pipe over the dahlias. He said the smoke kept the earwigs away, and he'd taken to coming out after tea every night on earwig patrol, but I saw Mum's face when she watched him through the kitchen window, lost in his own thoughts, and I knew he was worrying about Uncle Johnny. We all were. We hadn't heard from him in months, and we didn't even know which ship he was on, let alone where he was posted.

I sat on the ground beside the wheelbarrow and watched the bees buzzing around the garden. Scamp tired of his game when he saw me sit down, and came to lie beside me with his head in my lap. It was only then that Daddy looked down and noticed me.

"Hello, Ducks," he said, stroking my hair. "Are you joining the Earwig Patrol?"

I held his hand. It was dry and warm and comforting.

"May I have one of your big paper bags, please, Daddy? The ones you use to keep the dahlias over winter? At school tomorrow, we're going out picking rosehips for rosehip syrup."

He knocked out his pipe on the edge of the wheelbarrow and stood up, pulling me up with him.

"Come on, then, let's have a look in the shed. And tell your teacher the best place to look for rosehips is along the river. The wild roses up there have been 'blooming' lovely this year."

He winked at me and laughed at his own pun, and we set off up the garden to find a bag.

~*~

Maureen was out of luck. We didn't go out looking for rosehips until after lunch, which meant she had to sigh and puff her way through mental arithmetic *and* a spelling test.

After lunch, Miss Williams lined us up in twos at the door, and off we went, marching up the lane and over the bridge to the wide river bank. I hadn't needed to give her Daddy's message; she knew where to look.

As we walked, some of the boys started singing, "Hi Ho, Hi Ho, it's off to work we go," from Snow White, which we'd all seen at the pictures, and the whole class joined in, even Miss Williams, although not everyone could do the whistling bit.

Then they went on to "Whistle While You Work," but singing the words we sang in the playground:

"Whistle while you work,
Hitler is a twerp,
He's half barmy,
So's his army,
Whistle while you work."

I glanced at Miss Williams. She wasn't singing along, but she was smiling, so she didn't mind us singing the rude version.

We came around a bend in the river and saw a strange sight: a tall man in a big floppy hat appeared to be standing on the water!

As we got closer, we could see that he was actually standing in a flat boat, balancing carefully as he swung a scythe to trim the grass along the edges of the river. All the drinking water for London came from that river, so it had to be kept free-running.

The man turned as he heard us marching along singing, and laughed when he heard the words, pushing his hat back from his face. It was Micky! We hadn't seen him in ages, and had assumed he'd moved away.

He saw me smiling at him and called out, "Well, if it isn't young Sylvie! What are you doing? Skipping school?" he winked at Miss Williams as he said it, and I introduced her to him, explaining who he was.

"We've come out to pick rosehips," I said.

"Well, you've come to the right place," he said, pointing along the river. "Just a few yards down there is a big patch of roses."

We carried on walking, waving goodbye to Micky, and sure enough, just round the next bend of the river were masses of rosehips.

We spread out along the hedge and started picking. The hedge had been cut back at the bottom so people could walk along the bank, so the best of the hips were high up.

Georgie "Dicky" Bird decided to climb up into a tree to pick the best and fattest hips, throwing them down to the rest of us, but when he came to get down he found a problem; he couldn't find the footholds he'd used to climb up.

"Miss! Miss!" he called, "I can't get down!"

Miss Williams came running. "Oh, George," she cried, "trust you!"

She stepped nearer to the tree and reached up. "Lean down as far as you can and take my hands."

Dicky whimpered, but did as she said, so he was perched on a branch, leaning some of his weight on her hands.

"Now, on three, jump, and I'll catch you round the waist and break your fall. Ready? One . . . two . . . three. . . ."

Dicky jumped, but he was a big boy, and not very agile, and as he fell he pushed Miss Williams backwards. She stepped back with her left foot as Dicky landed safely, and her foot went down a hole in the ground. She fell sideways and sat heavily with a yell.

"Ow! My ankle!"

We rushed forward and several people tried to help her up.

"Wait, wait. Everyone step back a moment and let me catch my breath." She shuffled round to get her feet out from under her and tried to stand up. "Ow!" she said again. "It's no good, I think I've twisted my ankle. I can't put weight on it." She beckoned one of the bigger boys over and leaned her weight on him to stand on her good leg. "What are we going to do? I can't send you all back to school on your own, and I can't sit here all night!"

I had an idea.

"Miss, I'll run back and fetch my friend Micky. He'll know what to do. I'll be quite safe; Maureen will come with me."

"Good idea, Sylvie," said Miss Williams, wincing as she tried to put her left foot to the ground. "I hope he's still there."

Maureen and I ran back to where we'd seen Micky. He had moved along the bank a little way, but he was still working away steadily.

"Micky!" I called. "We need your help! Miss Williams has hurt her foot and can't walk. How are we going to get her back to school?"

Micky put the scythe down in the boat and stood thinking, then he picked up a long pole from the bottom of the boat, took the mooring rope in his hand, and carefully stepped off the boat. He tied the rope firmly to a ring set into the side of the riverbank and, with the pole in his hand, he followed me back along the bank to where Miss Williams stood, clinging to a tree.

"Oh, dear me, Miss, that's going to swell up nicely if we don't get you home soon. Here, use this pole as a stick and I'll walk on the other side of you."

Miss Williams gripped the pole and hopped forward on her good foot, Micky holding her elbow on the other side of her. As they slowly made their way along the path, she noticed Micky limping and looked sideways at him.

Micky laughed. "Oh, I'm not mocking you, Miss. I have a bad leg, meself."

"He hurt it when he worked in the circus, Miss!" I piped up.

Miss Williams raised an eyebrow at him and he shrugged his shoulders and laughed.

Slowly, step by step, we made our way back to school. Dicky, feeling bad about having caused the accident, ran ahead when we came to the playground and trotted to the office to fetch Miss Manning.

We steered Miss Williams into the classroom and Micky helped her into her chair.

Miss Manning followed an anxious Dicky into the room.

"Miss Williams! Are you all right?" She thanked Micky for his help and knelt to take Miss Williams' shoe off her injured foot. Her ankle was swollen and red.

"I think we need to get you home and get some ice on that ankle, Miss Williams. Class Three, you may go home early. Please explain to your parents that Miss Williams has had a slight accident, but she will be fine, and school will continue as usual tomorrow. I will teach you until Miss Williams is better."

Micky knelt down and took Miss Williams' hand.

"May I pop in to school when you're back and see how you're doing?" he asked.

"That's very kind of you, Mr. . . . ."

"Call me Micky," he said, standing up and shaking Miss Manning's hand. "I'm glad young Sylvie had the sense to come and get me. She's a good girl." He ruffled my hair. "Tell your parents I'll be round to see them when I finish work." He tipped his hat to the teachers and limped away.

Dicky and his friends ran out behind Micky, delighted to finish school an hour early.

"Miss has got a boooyyyyfrieeend!" he chanted.

Miss Williams blushed and laughed.

Chapter Fifteen

I Promise To Do My Best

I tied my golden yellow tie slowly and carefully. Fold the big square into a triangle, roll it evenly from the point and make it into a long flat tube about two inches across. Then fold up about one third; that was tricky, guessing a third. Putting my tongue out helped.

Now the really difficult bit; fold the long end round the short end, and back through its own loop. Done! I looked proudly at my tidily folded tie lying on the bed. I'd done it a few times now, but had never been as nervous as last week in front of all the other Brownies and Brown Owl, tying my tie for my tenderfoot test.

I picked up the loose ends and tied them at the back of my neck under the collar of my brown dress. The dress was a bit big. It had been passed on by one of the Brownies who had "flown up" to the Girl Guides, but Mum said it might last me out, if I didn't grow too much.

By the end of the evening, I would have a shiny oval badge to pin to my tie that said I was a real Brownie, and a Six badge to sew on to my dress.

As I laced up my school shoes, I ran over the words of the Brownie Promise in my head again and again. I mustn't make a mistake in front of the whole pack!

A tapping sound on my bedroom wall, two long taps followed by two short taps, meant that Maureen was ready. The taps were our code for, "Ready. Coming?"

Mum and Mrs Fielding sometimes used our tapping code

through the kitchen wall if they were going somewhere together and it was too cold to stand around on doorsteps.

I tapped back the same rhythm and ran down the stairs.

"Sylvie?" called Mum from the kitchen. "Don't forget I'll be out at the Mothers' Union when you get back. Have you got your key? Daddy's having tea at Grandma's on his way home from work, so you might need to let yourself in when you get back."

I rummaged in the many pockets of my Brownie uniform and pulled out a length of string, a pencil, pennies for making a telephone call in an emergency, a notepad, a clean hanky, and . . . my door key.

I'd been given my own key when I turned seven, and now I was allowed to go out to play on my own after tea, and go and call for friends, as well as doing shopping errands in the village at weekends. I felt very grown up, having my own key.

"Come here and let me look at you," said Mum. I stood to attention and gave the Brownie Salute, holding my first two fingers up, my thumb holding the other two down, and my palm facing outwards. It was a bit like Mr Churchill's salute, but with the fingers together. I wasn't really allowed to salute until I made my Promise, but I needed to practise it!

Mum straightened my tie and patted my shoulder.

"Very smart, dear. Now off you go, and have fun, my little Pixie!"

~*~

Maureen was at her front gate waiting, looking miserable. She looked even more miserable when she saw me in my new uniform. She wasn't going to be making her Promise this evening, as she hadn't passed her Tenderfoot test yet. She still hadn't mastered using her tie as a sling, and she kept getting the second verse of the National Anthem wrong. I'd been helping her, even though she wasn't in my Six, but she still stumbled over "Frustrate their knavish tricks" in the second verse.

She wasn't very good at her Six's song, either, but she was in the Imps, and their song was a bit silly.

"We're the ever-helpful Imps,
Quick and quiet as any shrimps!"

Who ever heard of a noisy shrimp, anyway? I suppose there's not much that rhymes with "Imps".

I was about to become an official Pixie, and our song was fun and made more sense.

"Look out, we're the jolly Pixies,
Helping people when in fixes!"

We talked about school all the way to the scout hut; at least I talked, Maureen just said "yes" and "no". She was sulking because I was going to be a proper Brownie before she was.

I gave up trying to chat as we came to the scout hut. Other girls were arriving too, and my Sixer, Joan, came over. She was ten years old and already in the Big Girls' school.

"Are you ready, Sylvie?" she asked. "Have you learned your Promise?"

I nodded and smiled. I wasn't sure whether it was right to salute her or not, so decided not to salute anyone until I had my Promise Badge.

Brown Owl was waiting for us in the hut and smiled as we came in in twos and threes.

Brown Owl was Miss Elsie Whitefield who lived at Park Grange where Auntie Maude worked. She wasn't really a proper Brown Owl; she was only seventeen and still in the Land Rangers, but her older sister, Miss Joan, now Mrs Flight Lieutenant Aldridge, who had been Brown Owl, had joined the WAAF, so Miss Elsie took over, with her youngest sister, Miss Daisy, who was fifteen, as Tawny Owl.

It had taken me a while to learn to call them Brown Owl and Tawny Owl and not Miss Elsie and Miss Daisy.

The Magic Carpet was laid out in the middle of the room,

with the Toadstools set on it in a ring. The Magic Carpet was an old rug from park Grange, and the Toadstools were made from papier maché and painted, but it looked really magical, like a proper fairy ring. This was the part I loved!

Brown Owl called us to attention, and we formed up in lines in our Sixes, with our Sixers standing at the front of each line of six Brownies. Brown Owl and Tawny Owl stood facing each other with their arms up, holding each other's hands above their heads to make an arch, and off we went, skipping around the hall, la-la-ing the Brownie song, and passing under the arch to form a circle around the carpet, then we all sang the words of the Brownie song together.

"We're the Brownies, here's our aim,
Lend a Hand and play the game"

"Before we dance around the toadstools," announced Brown Owl, "we have a new Brownie who is going to make her Promise this evening. Sylvia Ford, please step forward."

This was it! I stepped out of the circle and marched to stand in front of Brown Owl. My hands felt clammy and my knees were shaking a bit. Everyone was looking at me, and I suddenly felt like I couldn't remember my own name, let alone my Promise.

Brown Owl smiled at me, made the Brownie Salute and mouthed "Breathe!"

I took a deep breath, saluted her back, and said loudly and firmly,

"I promise to do my best:
To do my duty to God and the King
To help other people every day,
Especially those at home."

Brown Owl smiled and nodded, then leaned forward and pinned my Promise Badge to my tie.

She handed me my cloth Six Badge, which I had to sew

onto my uniform myself, and shook hands with me left handed, in the proper Brownie way.

I was a real Brownie!

I floated through our Six's dance around the carpet, thinking of all the exciting things I would do now I was a Brownie. Camping, cook-outs, learning lots of new things, and keeping my promise to be helpful.

~*~

I was still floating on the way home, but decided to start being helpful by getting Maureen word perfect on the National Anthem. We sang it over and over all the way home, until she got it right.

"But I still can't put someone's arm in a sling," she said sadly.

"You can!" I encouraged her. "You've done it right when we were practising; you just got nervous in front of Brown Owl and fumbled it. Next time, you'll pass."

It was starting to get dark, so we said goodnight. I nearly saluted her, but thought better of it. She wasn't a proper Brownie like me yet.

~*~

I unlocked the front door and switched on the light. Audrey was at the Mothers' Union meeting with Mum, and Daddy wasn't home yet. Scamp came running to meet me and I gave him a head scratch and a cuddle. The house was very quiet; the only sound was the clock in the front room ticking.

I took my Brownie Handbook from the sideboard drawer and settled down cross-legged on the rug to read all the things a Brownie should know.

Suddenly, there was a clatter in the lean-to, and Daddy's voice called, "Amy? Come quick!"

I ran through to the kitchen. Daddy was struggling to open the back door one-handed, and I saw that he had his hanky wrapped round his left hand, and it was soaked in blood!

"Daddy! What happened? Mummy's not home yet."

"It's nothing much, Sylvie, don't panic," he said. "I came off my bike; I hit a pothole in the road in the dark and scraped my hand on a wall when I fell. It's just a scrape, not deep, but it won't stop bleeding. Be a good girl and get me a bandage, then run to the church hall and fetch Mummy. I can't strap it up one-handed."

I thought quickly, then ran to the wall and tapped. Three fast taps, then another three, meaning, "Come round, now!"

I hoped Maureen had heard.

I unpinned my Promise Badge and took off my tie, shaking it out, then I took my clean hanky from my pocket and wrapped it round the cut on the back of Daddy's hand, pulling it tight.

Maureen ran in the back door, looking worried.

"What's the matter?" she puffed.

"We need to get Daddy's arm in a sling," I said. "Remember what Brown Owl said? If something's bleeding, you need to hold it up, so the blood has to work harder to get there. I'll hold the bandage on while you tie the sling."

"But . . . but. . . ." stammered Maureen.

"Maureen! You can *do* it!"

Maureen snatched up the tie, folded it diagonally, muttering to herself, and tucked it under Daddy's arm, then pulled the points up and tied them at the back of his neck. It was a perfect sling!

I peeped under the sling at the bandage. It looked all right. I couldn't see any blood coming through.

The front door opened and we heard Mum and Audrey wiping their feet on the mat.

"Hello? Anyone home? How did it go. . . ."

Mum stopped stock still in the kitchen door.

"Tom! Whatever happened?" She dropped her bag and hurried over.

"Don't worry, Ducks, I'm all right," Daddy reassured her. "I just came off my bike in the dark and scraped my hand. It was bleeding a lot, but these two Brownies here have done a good first aid job on me."

"Let me get my coat off and I'll strap it up properly; it needs washing, in case you've got any dirt in there, but I have to say you girls made a very good job of that bandage and sling! Well done!"

"Maureen tied the sling," I said. "She got it right first time."

Just then, there was a knock at the front door. I ran to open it while Mum helped Audrey out of her coat and Maureen filled the kettle to make a cup of tea.

Brown Owl was standing at the door with my knitted Brownie hat in her hand.

"Hello, Sylvie," she said. "I found your hat when I was tidying the hall. You must have forgotten it in the excitement."

Daddy had followed me to the door to see who the visitor was, and Brown Owl gasped when she saw his arm in a sling.

"Goodness, Mr Ford, what happened to you?"

"It's not as bad as it looks, Miss Elsie," he replied, "just a messy graze, but thanks to your teaching, these two efficient little Brownies looked after me well."

"Maureen did the sling all by herself, Brown Owl!" I pointed out.

"She did," agreed Daddy, "and a very neat job it is, too!"

He turned round and bent at the knees so she could inspect the knot at the back of his neck.

"Well done, Maureen!" said Brown Owl. "As you have an adult to confirm that you did this by yourself in a genuine emergency, I am going to pass you on that part of your tenderfoot test. If you bring your book to me at the start of the next meeting, I'll sign it off for you, and then maybe we can tackle that National Anthem test too."

"Thank you, Brown Owl!" Maureen beamed. "I'm sure I can sing the second verse properly, now; Sylvie helped me learn it on the way home."

"Well done, Brownies!" said Brown Owl, and saluted.

We both saluted back, even though Maureen wasn't really supposed to yet, but she was so nearly a Brownie now that it didn't matter.

Part Five
1943

Chapter Sixteen

There Were Never Such Devoted Sisters

My satchel came right down to Audrey's knees. She was three and a half years younger than me and a good foot shorter.

I showed her how to adjust the buckle on the strap to make it a better length and slung my own shiny new satchel over my head and shoulder.

It wasn't new-new, but it had come out of a super surprise package that arrived for us just before Christmas. The box was from Mum's Great Aunt Carrie, who lived in America. I didn't know Mum had a Great Aunt Carrie, and Mum said she'd almost forgotten, herself!

Aunt Carrie was Mum's grandma's youngest sister, and she had a daughter Lydia who was around Mum's age and size, and two granddaughters, Marleen and Shirleen, who were a little bit bigger than Audrey and me. I didn't think Marleen and Shirleen were proper names, but Mum said they were American, and what did we know, anyway.

In the box were tins of meat: pork, chicken, and beef; packets of dried fruit; more fruit in tins; tea, coffee, and biscuits; and, best of all, clothes!

There were shirts for Daddy, stockings and a dress for Mum, two beautiful wool school dresses that were just a little bit big for Audrey and me, board games, and a shiny leather satchel that Mum said I could have as the elder sister.

My satchel was passed down to Audrey, and inside it there were now three names written in indelible pencil;

~~Amelia Shepherd~~
~~Sylvia Ford~~
Audrey Ford

The very best thing of all in that Christmas box was hanging upstairs in the wardrobe I shared with Audrey; a beautiful pale blue georgette party dress that fitted me perfectly. It was draped in a sheet to keep it clean, but every now and again I would lift the sheet just to look at that wonderful dress. I hoped I'd have an occasion to wear it before I grew out of it.

Mum locked the front door and turned to us with a smile.

"Be good, both of you," she said, looking us up and down. "Audrey, do what your teacher tells you, and listen hard. After school, wait for Sylvie. You can walk home together until you get used to it and find your own friends to walk with."

She kissed us quickly and set off to catch her bus to work.

There was no sign of Maureen, so I opened and shut her front gate with a loud click, a sound that she would know meant "Hurry up!"

"Hello Audrey!" We turned round and there were the twins, Brenda and Beryl Skinner, crossing the road with their little brother, Brian. "Are you starting school today, Audrey?" asked Beryl, or Brenda, I never could tell.

Audrey nodded, her eyes huge, and stared at Brian.

"That's good, isn't it Aud," I said, nudging her to make her speak. "You'll know someone in your class." Audrey said nothing.

"Oh, is it a convoy?" laughed Maureen, joining us at last and slamming the door behind her.

~*~

We ran down the road together, us four older ones chatting away about what we'd done over the Christmas holidays, and Audrey and Brian in complete silence almost until we got to the school gate.

Then Brian suddenly said, "I've got marbles in my satchel. You can play, if you like."

Audrey looked up at me and I nodded enthusiastically at her. "That's nice, Aud, you've already got something to do at playtime!"

She looked at Brian and said nothing.

Miss Eames was already in the playground, ready to collect the after-Christmas starters in Class One, so we left the little kids with her and lined up with our own class.

I looked across at Audrey as we marched in. She was still silent. No tears, she didn't look unhappy, but I was worried.

~*~

At playtime, I stayed behind a few minutes, collecting up paintbrushes and arranging them in their glass jar on the bench by the door. Through the classroom door, I could see the playground, and the little ones from Class One were running out, yelling and laughing.

"Come on, Sylvie, aren't you coming out?" nagged Maureen.

"In a minute," I muttered, fiddling with the brushes and watching the playground from the corner of my eye. There was Audrey, running out . . . with Brian! And she was talking to him! I let out a big sigh of relief.

"Come on, then." I grabbed Maureen's hand and we ran out to join the rest of the girls in our class skipping with a long rope.

By lunchtime, the skipping rope had been confiscated. Maureen had decided to play a game where she held the rope by one handle and whirled round on the spot, and the rest of us had to jump over the rope as it whipped round on the ground.

It was all going well until one of the new kids in Class One walked into the flying wooden handle and started howling.

The rope was now in Miss Williams' desk until the end of school.

Audrey was running around playing "It" with some of the others in her class, and hadn't been near me all day, except for a quick wave in the dining room. And she had eaten all her lunch, including the carrots. Wait till I told Mum.

"One, two, three, four...," I counted, throwing the ball under my leg up against the wall and catching it again.

"I know why you were hanging around at playtime," said Maureen.

I stopped counting and stood still.

"Why, then?" I asked.

"You didn't want Audrey hanging round with us, did you?" Before I had a chance to answer she carried on, "I'm pleased you did that. I mean, she's a nice kid and all that, but we don't want little kids tagging along, do we?"

"No," I said. "You're right, we don't want little ones around."

I smiled to myself as I carried on with the game. "Five, six, oh, blast!" I fumbled the last catch and it was Maureen's turn.

She snatched the ball, and started her set of sevens by throwing the ball straight against the wall and catching it.

"If you said "blast" in front of Audrey, she'd tell your mum," she said, over her shoulder. "We're better off without her."

I settled back against a tree to watch her. She didn't have any brothers or sisters and wouldn't understand how worried I'd been that Audrey would be miserable.

~*~

I was looking forward so much to the afternoon; we were going to start learning to write proper joined-up writing with ink pens.

Mum had a beautiful ink pen that she said was made from Bakelite. It was black, with bright green swirls in the handle, and when she filled it to write letters or Christmas cards, she unscrewed the bottom half of the handle, dipped the nib into the ink bottle, and pulled a tiny lever inside the pen to fill it with ink. There was a propelling pencil that matched the pen; the tiny thin lead went right the way down the pencil, and you twisted the join at the middle to make the lead come out, so you never had to sharpen it.

Mum said that if I got into the Grammar School, she and Daddy would buy me a pen and pencil set like that.

The pens we used in class weren't so exciting or comfortable to hold. They were old-fashioned metal nibs set into plain wooden handles, and the handles were blobbed and stained with ink, but writing with a smooth metal nib instead of a pencil that kept breaking was heaven! I made a blobby mess at first, but by the end of the afternoon I was almost in a trance, swooping my pen across the smooth "best" paper and forming rows of perfectly shaped, joined-up "a"s and "o"s.

~*~

As we packed away our things, I carefully put the cap back on the inkwell and rested my pen in the special groove at the back of the desk, thinking all the while about how good it would be to move up to the Big Girls' school in September. One step closer to Grammar School and my prize pen!

Maureen was chattering away as we walked out of school, and I was still daydreaming about going to a school where I had to wear a uniform with a hat. . . .

"Oh!" I stopped dead and grabbed Maureen's arm.

"What?" she asked. "Have you got a stone in your shoe?"

I gaped at her. "What? No! *Audrey*!"

We turned and ran as fast as we could back to school. How could I have forgotten my little sister? My only little sister!

As we turned the corner by the park, we saw a tall figure walking towards us, holding Audrey by the hand and laughing at some long story she was telling him. Micky saves the day again!

He had taken to turning up after school a lot lately, sometimes to meet me and walk me home, but more often to walk Miss Williams home, although we were "big enough and ugly enough", as Mum said, to walk home by ourselves, especially Miss Williams!

We ran up to the pair of them, and I looked at Audrey. She didn't seem the slightest bit upset until she saw me, then she looked guilty.

"Oh, Sylvie! I forgot I was supposed to wait for you! Please don't tell Mummy!"

Micky cleared his throat and looked at me with one eyebrow quirked up. I wished I could do that.

"I'm sure Sylvie wouldn't be so mean as to tell tales that someone forgot to wait for her sister," he said, with meaning in his voice and a twinkle in his eye.

I looked at him gratefully. "No, of course I won't tell, Audrey," I said, and took her other hand as we walked home together.

Chapter Seventeen

"I Do" And Mend

"I can't wait till this war is over and I can have some new clothes," Maureen whined, picking uselessly at the stitching of a dress hem.

"Maureen Fielding!" her mum cried, horrified. "How dare you be so ungrateful! All those men, including your Dad, out there fighting, and Mrs Ford and the girls letting us come round so they can help us with all these alterations. You should be ashamed of yourself, young lady!"

Maureen carried on picking at the hem, muttering under her breath.

We had a production line running. I was perched on the windowsill writing on name tape with an indelible pencil; Maureen was supposed to be unpicking old name labels and hems; Mrs Fielding was pinning in new labels and placing binding round the hems of dresses to be lengthened, her mouth full of pins; Mum was at the kitchen table with the Singer, stitching away; and Audrey was taking the pins out of the stitched hems and pushing them into a pincushion to be used again.

We had to do Gym at the Big Girls', which meant gymslips, gym knickers, and Aertex shirts, all needing name tapes, and anything else we were likely to wear to school had to have name tapes stitched in, too.

Maureen and I had both been handed down gym clothes from older girls who had grown out of them. Norma across the road had given hers to Maureen, and mine had belonged to my Brownie Sixer, Joan.

Bottletops For Battleships

Mum decided to make a day of it on the first Saturday of the summer holiday and have a fitting session, letting down all our dresses, and where they'd already been let down she was adding contrast bands round the bottom to lengthen them further. Any long sleeves that were too short in the arm were cut and hemmed into short sleeves.

Daddy had given up and gone to Grandma's to cut her grass for her; it was all too busy and feminine for him.

I looked up from my endless printed capitals "SYLVIA FORD SYLVIA FORD" on the name tape and glanced out of the window. The breeze was blowing the curtain in, and carrying a rich Irish voice in with it. The voice was saying, "I can't wait to see her face!" and a female voice laughed.

Footsteps came up the front path and I ran to open the door for Micky and . . . Miss Williams!

"Are ye going to invite us in, or just stand there gawping?" he asked cheekily, and chucked me under the chin. I stepped back and let them in, silently. It felt weird having my old teacher visiting my house.

"Micky!" Mum came running from the kitchen, picking loose threads off her dress. "And Miss Williams, how lovely! Sylvie, go and put the kettle on."

"Actually, it was Sylvia we came to see," said Miss Williams, smiling. She looked at Micky and then shyly down at the floor.

"We've got some news. We're going to be married. The banns will be read on Sunday. We wanted to come and tell all of you first, especially Sylvie, as it was Sylvie who introduced us that day I twisted my ankle." We all gasped and congratulated them. So that's why Micky kept coming up to the school!

"And," continued Miss Williams, "as I don't have any sisters or girl cousins, I'd like you to be my bridesmaid, if you'd like to, Sylvie?"

I stood stock still, my mouth open.

"Is that a yes?" laughed Micky.

"Oh, yes! Yes, please!" I felt like hugging Miss Williams, but didn't quite like to hug a teacher, even if she wasn't my own teacher any more.

"I don't know what we'll find you to wear, but we'll think of something," she said.

"I know!" I ran up the stairs and flung the wardrobe door open. I lifted the sheet cover off carefully and carried my beautiful georgette dress gently down the stairs, looping the skirt over my arm.

"I could wear this, Miss Williams. Do you like it?"

"Oh Sylvie!" she cried. "It's beautiful! And with you wearing that, that's my "something blue" solved! Now I just need something old, something new, and something borrowed!"

We all laughed and Mum moved a pile of clothes off the settee so the engaged couple could sit down.

"Now then, Miss Bridesmaid, what about that tea?"

"Will your parents be coming up from Wales for the wedding, Miss Williams?" asked Mrs Ford.

"I'm hoping my mother can come," Miss Williams replied. "My dad died three years ago, but my brother's going to give me away, if he can get leave. He's a Bevin Boy down the mines."

"If he can't get away, I'm sure my Tom would be delighted to do the honours," said Mum.

"Then you'll have the something borrowed!" chirped Audrey, cheekily. She was much more confident about talking to people since she started school.

"And what about Kattie?" asked Mum. "Have you told her, Micky?"

"Oh, my Ma's delighted, so she is," said Micky, squeezing his bride-to-be's hand. "She can't believe I found brains *and* beauty!"

Miss Williams blushed and smacked him lightly on the arm.

"What about your dress?" asked Maureen. "Do you get extra coupons for getting married?"

"No," laughed Miss Williams, "but I've saved some up, so I might be able to get something decent."

"Don't you worry about that, my angel." Micky winked and tapped the side of his nose. "I know where I can get some beautiful white silk for my bride."

"And I've got boxes and boxes of patterns upstairs, and I'm more than willing to help you make your dress," said Mum.

"Oh, that's kind of you," Miss Williams beamed. "I can sew, but it's so hard fitting a dress on yourself, isn't it!"

~*~

I must have been asleep a good half an hour when the knock came at the front door. I looked at my folding alarm clock and it showed nine o'clock! Whoever was visiting at this time of night?

I crept to the top of the stairs, avoiding the creaky board outside the spare room, and hid behind the newel post to see what was going on.

Mum was standing at the door talking to another lady; I could only see her bottom half from where I was crouched; and they were looking at a silvery river of material that was spilling from the lady's hands and shining under the hall light.

"Oh, it's beautiful!" gasped Mum.

"And it's not parachute silk or anything, really it isn't!" said the other voice. Miss Williams!

"I know a lot of people think Michael's a spiv, and they don't believe in his leg injury, but he's told me the story behind how he got this silk. It was a gift a good few years ago from a friend who he . . . did a good turn for. That's why I'm bringing it round this late; I didn't want anyone to see me with it and start gossiping. . . ." She trailed off, sounding worried.

"It's all right, dear, I know the story of how Micky got his injury. His mother told me years ago, though he doesn't know that I know. And anyone spreading gossip about that good man will have me to answer to! A spiv, indeed! I'll put this safely in my wardrobe drawer and we'll see you on Friday evening for a fitting. I've nearly got the toile of the bodice finished out of that old piece of sheet."

"Thank you, Mrs Ford. I'll see you then. You're all so kind. I know Michael's not related to you, either, but I really feel like one of the family."

I slipped back to bed and lay thinking. What did Mum mean, how Micky got his injury? He'd told us, it was falling from the high wire in the circus! There was something mysterious going on here. I felt a strange cold feeling in my stomach. Maybe Micky wasn't who he said he was. Why was Miss Williams so worried about what people thought of her silk, and what was the good turn that Micky had done for a friend? He was always doing good turns for us, so it must have been a special one to be given such a lovely piece of material.

I couldn't ask Mum, or she'd know I'd been eavesdropping.

I tossed and turned a good while, wondering and worrying, but must have dropped off eventually, as I dreamed all night about a tightrope walker wearing a silk wedding dress.

~*~

The day of the wedding was fine and dry, but not sunny. Miss Williams and her mother came to our house early so they could get dressed, and Daddy went off to Micky's lodgings to keep him calm. Miss Williams' brother, David, had sent a telegram to say he was coming, but Daddy was on standby to give Miss Williams away if David didn't make it.

I was in a grumpy mood. Mum had decided I should have ringlets for the wedding so I'd spent the night trying to find a way to lay my head so a curl rag wasn't digging into my scalp, and I hadn't slept well.

"Sylvie, why don't you go down the garden and pick some sweet peas for Miss Williams' bouquet," said Mum, sighing as she moved me out from under her feet again. "And take Audrey and Scamp with you, please."

Audrey was going to the wedding, with Mum, but just as a guest, so she didn't have to have her hair tortured. I couldn't wait till those rags came out.

We clattered back into the kitchen a while later to find the most beautiful bride standing there! Miss Williams didn't look like herself at all. The dress was very simple: a long-sleeved dress with a sweetheart neckline and a bias-cut skirt that came to just below her knees. It didn't have a train, which left me with nothing to do except follow her and hold her flowers while she got married, but it looked lovely. She was wearing the shoes that her mother had worn when she got married, so that was her something old, her dress was new, and she had a little brooch in the shape of an Irish leprechaun sitting on a lucky horseshoe pinned on her dress; it was mine, and I was lending it to her just in case her brother made it on time and she didn't need to borrow Daddy.

The "blue" was hanging on the back of the kitchen door – my beautiful dress.

"Right then, Miss Bridesmaid," said Mum. "Take yourself off into that bathroom and have a lick and a promise, then we'll pop you into your dress and get those curls combed out. Come on, Audrey, let's wash your hands and face at the sink while Sylvie's primping in the bathroom."

Daddy popped his head round the front door. "Everybody decent?" he asked as he came in.

"Well!" He smiled. "I'm going to be very proud to walk down the street with five such fine ladies!"

He took Mrs Williams' arm on one side, and the bride's on the other, and I followed along with Mum and Audrey. It was only a short walk to the church: up to the top of the road and across the main street.

~*~

Mum led Audrey in to find a seat and Miss Williams and I waited in the porch with Daddy. We all kept looking up the road towards the station, hoping to see Miss Williams' brother coming running down the street, but all too soon the organ started up with "Here Comes The Bride" and Miss Williams sighed.

Daddy took her hand and tucked it into his elbow and patted it. "Ready?" he said, and in we glided.

Micky looked so handsome in his brown suit, I almost didn't recognise him! He looked overcome when he saw his beautiful bride, who couldn't stop beaming.

The service went on a bit, with a lot of talking in between the hymn singing, so I amused myself by looking at the ladies' hats.

Mrs Fielding had been very clever with her hat. It was an old straw hat that she wore when she was working on the allotment, but she had painted it tan, turned up one side of the brim, and pinned it with a little brooch with a green stone, and added some brown feathers. With her green wool suit and her best tan shoes and bag, it looked very stylish.

The last hymn started up, and we all stood to sing, "The Lord's My Shepherd". As the organ wheezed out the tune and the nearly all female congregation trilled the words, there suddenly came a rich, deep man's voice from the back door of the church. I saw Miss Williams' shoulders tense, as though she was frozen on the spot, then as we all turned towards the door a young, slim, dark-haired man walked briskly down the aisle, singing in that beautiful voice all the while, and caught up his sister in a big hug. He shook hands energetically with Micky, still singing, then slid into a pew beside his mother, who was wiping her eyes for the second time.

We walked in procession to the scout hut for the reception, the new Mr and Mrs Connolly leading the way, followed by Daddy and Mrs Williams, then Mum with David Williams, and Audrey and me bringing up the rear of the bridal party, with the rest of the guests following along behind.

As we tucked into our spam sandwiches and tinned fruit salad in jelly, the happy couple circled the room, talking to everyone in turn.

Miss . . . Mrs Connolly stooped down to pin my leprechaun brooch back on my dress.

"Thank you, dear Sylvie, for being such a good bridesmaid," she said as she kissed me. "You were so calm, you stopped me from being nervous!"

"You look so beautiful, Mrs Connolly," I said.

"I think as I'm practically family, you should call me Helen now," she suggested.

"I think maybe Auntie Helen might be more suitable," said Mum, "and of course, Audrey, you must say 'Mrs Connolly' at school."

"So long as nobody's going to start calling me 'Uncle'!" laughed Micky, and we all joined in. Micky wasn't serious enough to be an uncle!

There was a small commotion at the door through to the tiny kitchen as Mrs Fielding appeared carrying the wedding cake.

It was beautiful! Three round, smooth white tiers, topped with a silver glass bell and a wreath of sweet peas.

Mrs Fielding placed the cake carefully on the table, and the newlyweds posed for a photograph for the local paper, Micky's big hands wrapped over Auntie Helen's on the knife, the blade gently touching the top tier of the cake but not breaking the icing.

Click! "Thank you, Mr & Mrs Connolly," said the photographer and bustled away. Out of the corner of my eye, I saw Mum stop him on his way out and talk to him for several minutes, looking very serious.

Mrs Fielding stepped forward to the cake and . . . lifted all that lovely icing off in one piece! It was cardboard!

The real wedding cake was a small sultana sponge cake that looked a bit lost, sitting on the huge cake board, but there was enough for everyone to have a small slice. In our house, we'd all given up sugar in our tea as soon as we heard about the wedding, so Mrs Fielding would have enough sugar from our rations to make the cake.

The bride and groom couldn't afford a honeymoon, and probably wouldn't have been able to get a travel permit anyway, so they stayed to the end of the evening, dancing with the rest of us. Even Audrey managed to join in The Lancers and galloped across the room with Micky, laughing her head off at him folding himself in half so he could dance with her.

We were listening to the wireless after tea when we heard footsteps on the front path and Auntie Helen's laugh. I ran to open the door and she and her husband walked in, arm in arm, Micky waving a copy of the local paper.

"Well, me cover's blown now, to be sure," he said, laughing, but looking slightly embarrassed. "I don't know who told tales on me, but my darling wife denies everything!" He winked at me and handed me the paper, folded open at a photo of the bride and groom "cutting" their cake.

"Read it out loud, Sylvie, while I cover me face in blushes," he instructed.

"Local Teacher Marries Irish hero," I read from the headline. We all looked at Micky in surprise and he waved me on.

"Local infant teacher Miss Helen Williams was married on Saturday to Mr Michael Connolly, native of Howth, Dublin in the Republic Of Ireland.

"Mrs Connolly, who is held in great affection by pupils past and present, and is Vice Chairwoman of the Townswomen's Guild, was married wearing a hand-made dress of antique white silk. The material was given to her husband by a grateful elderly neighbour after he saved both her and her possessions from a fire, during which his leg was badly injured.

"It is understood that the silk was intended for the elderly lady's own wedding dress, but her fiancé was killed in the last war, so she gave it to her rescuer for his future bride.

"The happy couple will continue to live in the area, where Mr Connolly, a master builder by trade, is well known for taking on any job to help his neighbours and further the local war effort. Mrs Connolly will continue to teach."

I stopped reading and gazed at Micky in admiration. What a hero!

"I wonder how the man from the paper got to hear that story?" mused Micky, looking sideways at Mum.

"Oh, these things get around," she said, with a mischievous smile.

"But I thought you hurt your leg in the circus!" cried Audrey, confused.

"And so I did," said Micky, crouching down stiffly to hug her. "This thing called life is just one big circus!" He laughed, and swung her up to the ceiling, the way he used to do with me when I was little.

Chapter Eighteen

One Of The Big Girls

Maureen and I felt very grown up and important as we left all our younger friends who were still going to our old infant school and crossed the road to take the footpath down the side of the churchyard to our new school, St James', otherwise known as The Big Girls'.

Audrey looked back over her shoulder with big eyes as I said goodbye; she hardly ever spoke to me during school playtimes, but now she looked at me as though I was leaving her for ever! I think she had enjoyed swanking about, having a big sister in the top class.

The nearer we came to school, though, the younger and smaller we felt. There were what seemed like hundreds of girls running, walking and cycling to school, most of them bigger than us. We were back to being the little ones again.

Some of the very biggest girls in the top class, who hadn't moved up to the Grammar School, were nearly fourteen and would be leaving school next summer to go to work, or to secretarial college. Maureen watched them with interest. She wanted to leave at fourteen and train to be a typist so she could work for her Uncle Bill's building firm, typing up estimates and such, but I knew Mum and Daddy wanted me to try for the scholarship to the Grammar School in the third year. We couldn't afford the fees for the Grammar School, but Daddy said we could manage the uniform, and we'd probably know someone who had old uniform to hand down, so I was going to try hard to work towards the scholarship exam and win a place.

It was strange to walk into an assembly full of just girls, and I felt a bit sad that I wouldn't see some of my boy friends from our old school any more unless we met up after school.

The teachers filed in and lined up across the front of the hall behind the headmistress as the rows and rows of girls stood up and stopped chattering, and one of the teachers was a man!

Miss Young, the headmistress, introduced her staff to the new first years, and it turned out that the man teacher was called Monsieur Dupont. I'd never met a foreign person before!

~*~

The first lesson of the day was almost like being back in Miss Williams' class: we labelled our notebooks with our names, copied down the school rules and timetable from the board, and each of us read aloud one by one to our teacher, Miss Sandys, while the rest of us wrote about what we did in the holiday. I had worried all summer that Big School was going to be so much harder than Infants', but this was easy!

Miss Sandys was a small, dainty, elderly lady who spoke very quietly, but somehow I had the feeling that she wouldn't take any nonsense. From the first time she murmured, "Excellent reading, Sylvia, and what neat handwriting!" I felt that I would work my hardest to please her, and do well in her class.

~*~

The playground felt very empty with no boys: no footballs flying through the air, no Dinky toys whizzing under your feet. Maureen and I and the younger girls ran about playing ball, hopscotch, skipping, and clapping games, but the older girls just sat around on benches chatting about boys, hair, films and clothes. Boring!

When we trooped noisily back to our classroom, flushed and refreshed from our exercise, Mrs Sandys had disappeared and Monsieur Dupont was sitting at her desk, ready to take us for an art lesson. I was looking forward to this, I loved drawing and painting. But before we could get started, one of the girls asked him where he was from, and he started telling us a long rambling story about how he had escaped from Belgium and come to England to be an airman and fight the Germans, and had been shot down in the Battle of Britain. He had been injured so badly that he couldn't go back to fighting, so he had decided to stay and, as he put it, "help this country recover from the war by educating her children."

It was very interesting, but I wanted to get on with the art lesson, and I couldn't see how us learning to speak French and draw would help the country recover.

He was a good teacher, though, and that first lesson, he taught us about something called perspective. He drew a picture on the board of a railway line disappearing into the distance, then told us to mark out a vanishing point on a piece of sugar paper and quickly draw a made-up scene in chalk, showing perspective. I got the hang of it quite easily, but Maureen did something wrong with her vanishing point and her railway line went uphill.

By lunchtime, I had very chalky hands, a smudge on my blouse cuff, and I was ravenous, but at this school we couldn't simply walk down a corridor to the hall for dinner. The school kitchen had been hit by a stick of incendiary bombs during the Blitz and the school couldn't afford to re-build it, so we all had to walk, in two sittings, down to the church hall, where the school cooks and the Mothers' Union served us up a lunch cooked in the small kitchen there.

The first course was delicious: a vegetable stew full of turnips, carrots and potatoes grown in the school vegetable garden, bulked out with lentils and split peas, but for afters we were served tapioca pudding. I hated tapioca. It was like eating a plate of frogspawn, and the little bit of jam we were allowed to mix in with it didn't make it taste any better, but with the school cooks standing over us and posters saying, "Waste Not, Want Not," all round the room, we had to finish every slithery mouthful. Yuck.

~*~

According to the timetables we had copied into the front of our notebooks, Monday afternoon's lesson for Class One was gym. We clattered into the cloakrooms at the back of the hall and claimed our pegs, all trying to get a corner hook so we had more bench space to spread out. We changed into our white Aertex shirts and our navy gym slips and pulled our heavy navy serge gym knickers on over our ordinary knickers, stuffed our school shoes into the wire baskets under the benches, and laced up our rubber-soled gym shoes. The whole cloakroom smelt of rubber from those shoes.

Maureen had heard from a cousin of hers who was in Class Three that the gym mistress, Miss Robbins, was very strict, and had no time for anyone who wasn't very fit or athletic, so we were slightly dreading our first gym lesson.

We were lined up, talking quietly, in the corridor and jumped in surprise when the staff room door was flung open and a tiny, wiry-looking woman aged about fifty yelled, "Class One! Marching on the spot, GO! Left, right, left, right. . . ."

It was a bit like being in the army, but this part was quite fun, so long as you knew you left from your right. Maureen stumbled on the wrong feet, but I nudged her and she soon sorted herself out.

We marched in step down the corridor and into the hall, where some apparatus had been set up: a long beam, suspended about two feet off the floor between two upright posts, a tall wooden box with inward sloping sides and a cushioned top, and five ropes hanging down from a track in the ceiling.

We didn't need to be told to be quiet. We were all silent, wondering what on earth we were going to be expected to do.

This was a bit different from playing bat and ball in the playground and running races on the school field.

Miss Robbins divided us into three groups of ten girls and showed us what she wanted us to do. One group was to practise balancing across the beam. We could work in pairs to start, one girl on the floor holding the hand of her partner on the beam to steady her until she felt confident enough to walk on her own.

Another group was to practise vaulting over the box; you had to take a long run up, then bounce on a springy wooden board, slam your hands on the top of the box and push yourself over in one leap to land upright on the mat the other side. That was the idea, anyway, but most of that group flopped on top of the box on their stomachs the first time they tried.

The third group, that Maureen and I had been put into, was to practise climbing the ropes.

When Miss Robbins blew her whistle, the first five of us were to shin up the rope as far as we could and stay there until she blew the whistle again, then we were to climb down hand over hand.

I was in the first group of five and flung myself at the rope, trying to grip it between my feet enough to be able to pull myself up with my hands. I climbed about halfway up the rope and was relieved when the whistle blew so I could get down again.

Maureen was in the next group, along with a tall, slim girl called Jasmine, who had obviously done this before. She shinned up the rope like a monkey, and let go with one hand to wave when she reached the top. Luckily, Miss Robbins was too busy watching her star pupil to notice as poor Maureen hurled herself as high up the rope as she could and clung on like grim death until the whistle blew and she could plop down onto the mat.

We stumbled out of the school gates, weary and dishevelled, our gym kit stuffed anyhow into our bags.

"Let's go to the sweet shop on the way home," suggested Maureen. I knew she'd used up all her coupons and I was pretty sure she didn't have any pocket money left either, as she'd bought a comic at the weekend, but I didn't say anything.

It was a special occasion, our first day at big school, so I would treat her this once.

"Come on, then," I challenged her, darting on ahead. "Race you! First one there pays!"

Part Six
1944

Chapter Nineteen

All The Nice Girls Love A Sailor

As I turned into the top of our road, Audrey came running towards me. "Sylvie, Sylvie!" she yelled. "There's a motorbike come to tea at our house!"

"Well, you'd better give it a cup of tea and a piece of cake then," I teased her. "Who do we know with a motorbike?"

"I don't know," she said, taking my hand as we walked. "I haven't been in yet. I waited for you."

"We'd better run then. Mummy'll be worrying why you're so late!"

We ran down the road, satchels bumping against our hips. Audrey's school turned out ten minutes before mine, so she should have been home already, laying the table for tea. She was still very shy with people she didn't know, so much so that she'd rather be told off for being late home than walk into a room where she knew there was a strange visitor.

The motorbike parked outside our house had seen better days; it was shabby and battered and it had a weird pod thing attached to the side of it that had two wheels of its own.

As we took off our shoes on the doormat, we could hear Mum talking to a man who had a very familiar voice. I knew him, but I just couldn't think who he was from the voice alone.

"Here they are," said Mum as we opened the hall door. The man was sitting on the settee, dressed all in white, with very short blond hair, and a leather jacket that looked as old as the bike outside was flung across the armchair.

For a minute I looked at the visitor blankly, then I recognised him. "Uncle Johnny!"

He jumped up from the settee and picked me up in a big hug, then turned to Audrey. "Do you remember me, Audrey?" he asked. "You were only two last time I saw you, now look at you! A big girl all grown up and going to school!" He held his arms out to her and Audrey gave him what I called her "other family" hug. It was the one she used for Grandma and the aunts and uncles who she didn't see very often, a quick hug and then a wriggle to get away.

"Is that your motorbike outside, Uncle Johnny?" I asked as Mum got up to make another pot of tea.

"Yes, I bought it off a chap who was being posted overseas; he was hanging around the docks when we landed, desperately trying to sell the thing. Do you like it? If you're good, I'll take you out for a spin in it; you and Audrey can both fit in the sidecar together." He winked at us and jerked his head towards the kitchen.

"Not until Sylvie's done her homework, they can't," came Mum's voice. Uncle Johnny grinned and nodded. He'd deliberately said we could go on the bike with him to get a rise out of Mum.

Daddy walked in the back door just as we were finishing laying the table. Uncle Johnny was telling us about the horrible dried food they had to eat on board ship, and how cramped it was where they slept.

"Hello, Tom!" He grinned at the surprise on Daddy's face.

"Well I'm blowed," laughed Daddy, grabbing his youngest brother's hand and clapping him on the back. "I knew you'd turn up like a bad penny eventually. How much leave have you got? Have you been to see Mother yet?"

"I've got two weeks' leave," said Uncle Johnny, "then I'm being posted down to the south coast for top secret training."

"Oh! What are you going to be training for?" asked Audrey.

"It's a secret, silly, so he doesn't know! And anyway, even if he did, he wouldn't be allowed to tell us. Careless Talk Costs Lives, Walls Have Ears, and all that."

"All I know is there's some big push planned," he said, helping Daddy out of his jacket and hanging it on the back of the kitchen door. "I don't know where and I don't know when, but the top brass are utterly sick of this Hitler and his bombs and blockades. Whatever this is will be big.

I haven't been to see Ma. She doesn't know I'm back yet. I'll drive up there after tea."

"Drive?" asked Daddy.

"Yes, come and see the Beast. . . ."

"After tea, it's getting cold!" Mum scolded, but with a smile.

~*~

Uncle Johnny helped Mum and Audrey with the washing up and drying while I went outside with Daddy to look at the motorbike.

"I don't know what your grandma's going to say when her baby boy turns up on her doorstep on this rattletrap," Daddy laughed, kicking at the front tyre. "I just hope he's got enough petrol in it to get it up that hill."

"Come in, you two," called Mum. "Uncle Johnny's brought us all presents! Come and see!"

Uncle was kneeling in the middle of the floor untying the strings of an enormous duffle bag.

He pulled something out and handed it to Mum.

"For the lady of the house, perfume." He smiled, and kissed her hand like they do on the films.

"Oh, aren't they lovely!" she cried, showing us all two little glass scent bottles in the shape of sailor boys. Each boy had a painted-on face and a painted-on sailor collar, and their wide flat hats with a little button on the top were the bottle lids, which unscrewed. One bottle held rose perfume and the other lavender.

"I got them in France on the way home," he said, "They're French sailor boys."

He pulled out a soft cloth bag and handed it to Daddy; inside was a brand new pipe and a big pouch of tobacco. Daddy was delighted; he had almost given up smoking his pipe, as he had nearly run out of tobacco and it was almost impossible to get. He had tried making his own from tobacco plants, but when he put the dried leaves in his pipe and lit them, it just made a big blue cloud of smoke, and he said it tasted awful.

The next package that came out of the duffel bag was lumpy, with pointed edges here and there. Uncle Johnny looked at Audrey and me and beckoned us forward.

"These are for you," he said, opening the bag and pulling out two beautiful toy sailing boats. One was blue, and on the side of the bottom part, which he said was called the hull, it had the words "Lady Sylvia" painted in white, and the other was green and had "Lady Audrey" written on it.

The white sails were made of fine cotton material, and had proper ropes holding them in place, which Uncle Johnny said were called sheets. Sailors had very odd words for things.

"Tomorrow, I'll take you to the park after tea and we'll sail your boats on the duck pond," he said. "The ducks won't know what to make of them!"

"Thank you, Uncle Johnny!" I beamed. "I love my boat!"

"So do I!" cried Audrey. "Thank you, Uncle Johnny!" And she ran to him and gave him the biggest hug I'd ever seen her give anyone.

"Well, now, brother of mine," said Uncle Johnny. "As it's getting a bit late for these young ladies to go out, how do you fancy coming for a spin on the Beast up to Ma's? I can drop you back home again afterwards."

Daddy laughed. "And of course that offer has nothing to do with wanting moral support when Mother sees that death trap you're riding!" He smiled, as he lifted his gardening jacket down from its peg.

"Nothing at all," laughed Uncle Johnny. "Oh, and you'll have to ride pillion. The kit bag has to go in the sidecar."

We followed them to the door and watched as Uncle Johnny steadied the bike on tiptoe while Daddy slung the bag into the sidecar and climbed on behind him.

At the fourth kick of the starter, the bike spluttered into life and they raced off down the street in a cloud of smoke.

I ran home so fast after school that I got in only a few minutes after Audrey, but I suspected that she'd been dawdling, telling her friend Brian all about her sailor uncle on the way home.

Uncle Johnny was teaching Audrey how to tie knots in the front room and I watched them for a while; I could already do some of the knots, as I'd had to learn them for my Tenderfoot test in Brownies, but some of them were very complicated and practical-looking. I made my mind up to ask him to show me them again, slowly, before his leave finished, in case any of them came in useful at Brownie camp in the school holidays.

Over tea, Uncle Johnny told us all kind of exciting stories about being in the Navy: the places the ship called at on its tour of duty, the tricks and pranks the sailors played on each other, and the strange foods and customs that they came across on their travels.

He stacked the plates and carried them to the sink to start the washing up, but Mum stopped him.

"Off you go, you three, and take Scamp with you, he needs a walk, but don't forget the girls have got school in the morning so I don't want them out late. Home by half past seven. On the dot!"

As we closed the gate, Audrey's little friend Brian appeared.

"Can Brian come, too?" she asked. "He wants to be in the Navy when he's grown up."

"Run quickly and ask your mum then, Brian," said Uncle Johnny, and perched on the front wall while we waited, to explain to us how to set the sails of our boats so that they'd catch the wind.

The duck pond was cool and quiet under the trees, the ducks sitting dozing around the edges, but there was enough breeze to make the boats move.

Uncle Johnny showed us how to lick our fingers and hold them up to see which way the wind was blowing. Whichever side of your finger got cold first, that was the side the wind was blowing from.

We unrolled the long strings attached to the front, sorry, bows, of our boats and set them gently in the water. Uncle Johnny found a long stick to push them with to get them started and they were off, skimming across the pond. We held onto the long strings to keep the boats from getting out of reach, and followed them round the edge of the pond. When they got to the other side, we lifted them out and ran back round to launch them again, Scamp running behind us and dodging among our legs.

The ducks were starting to wake up and get interested in the noise and commotion. One big drake waddled to the edge of the pond, stepped into the water with a splash, and waggled his way across to the Lady Audrey. The other Audrey was jumping up and down on the bank, yelling at the duck to leave her boat alone, and in the excitement she forgot to hang onto her string. The boat, nudged by the duck, drifted across to the other side of the pond, which was edged with thick bushes, and came to a halt lodged against a piece of fallen tree branch. Audrey's bottom lip started to wobble.

"Don't worry, Audrey," said Uncle Johnny, taking off his boots and rolling up his trousers. "The pond's only a few inches deep. I'll wa. . . ." Before he finished the sentence, we heard a splash, and there was Brian, wading up to his knees across the pond to rescue the little boat. Scamp thought that was a great idea, and immediately plunged in behind Brian, but having short legs, his feet didn't touch the bottom so he had to swim doggy paddle.

Brian had reached the boat and we watched as he bent down to untangle the string from whatever it was caught round under the water. Scamp was determined to be in on the heroic rescue too, and thrashed about in the water, getting closer and closer. We could all see what was going to happen, but no-one had a chance to say more than "Brian!" before Scamp collided with the bending boy and knocked him face down in the water.

Poor Brian surfaced, spluttering water from his mouth and nose, his hair and clothes covered in slimy weed. Audrey started laughing. Uncle Johnny and I tried to shush her, but she was laughing so much we couldn't help joining in, and in the end even Brian was laughing fit to bust.

He waded back across the pond and handed the boat to Audrey, who was laughing so much I thought she might wet herself, and Uncle Johnny put out a hand to pull the soggy boy out of the pond.

Scamp was still thrashing around in the weeds, chasing the unfortunate duck who had caused all the trouble. Uncle Johnny whistled to him and called, "Come in, number nine, your time is up!" which set Audrey off again, and Scamp decided he'd had enough of a good thing and paddled back across the pond.

He scrambled out of the water and stood dripping, wagging his tail and looking at all of us. A gleam appeared in his eye; Uncle Johnny and I both realised at the same time what he was thinking and tried to step back out of his way, but it was too late. With one vigorous shake of his whole body, he covered those of us who weren't already wet with green smelly water and slimy weed.

~*~

We must have made a comical sight as we walked home; one completely soaking boy, ditto dog, two damp girls carrying toy boats, and a sailor in a lovely white uniform that was covered in green splashes.

"You two go in and start explaining to your mum, while I go and talk to Brian's mum," said Uncle Johnny, opening the front gate for us. Audrey and I looked at each other and sighed as I lifted the door knocker. Scamp just wagged his tail, making us even wetter.

I'd never seen Mum speechless before.

"What the. . . ?" she exclaimed, before running to lay old newspaper through the front room so the three of us could drip our way to the kitchen.

~*~

By the time Uncle Johnny came back, Mum was subsiding into giggles and wiping her eyes on her apron, and Daddy was chuckling at the story over his pipe, making it bubble every time he laughed.

The sight of Uncle Johnny, his resplendent uniform covered with green slime, set Mum off again into hysterical laughter.

Uncle Johnny stood on the doorstep, looking rueful.

"I won't come in," he said. "You've got enough mess to deal with already. Er, Tom, I don't suppose you fancy paying a visit to Ma this evening? I'll bring you back again. . . ?"

"Oh no," laughed Daddy, "you're on your own this time, little brother!"

Chapter Twenty

D Day

The playground was buzzing on Tuesday morning. No-one was running or playing; they were all standing around in little huddles, talking.

Maureen and I went up to the twins, who were holding forth importantly about something, working like a team, one talking while the other nodded agreement, and then swapping over.

"What's happened?" I asked when they both paused for breath at the same time.

"Don't you *know*?" they cried together.

I sighed.

"Well, no, obviously, or I wouldn't be asking, would I?"

"Oh! It was on the news this morning. We're invading Europe!" said Brenda.

We didn't listen to the morning news at home; with four of us to get washed, dressed, fed and out of the house, we only really had about ten minutes when we were all sitting together at the kitchen table, and Mum said that was family time, for us to talk about what we were doing and wish each other a good day.

As Daddy said, "The things on the news have happened, whether I know about them or not. They can wait till after tea."

"All the allies are working together: the navy, the army, the air force, the Americans, everyone," said Beryl. "They landed on the beaches in France in the night and they're fighting the Germans back. Isn't it exciting?!"

I didn't reply. I was thinking about what Uncle Johnny had said, just six weeks ago, about being posted to the south coast for top secret training. Maybe he was out on the sea in his ship right now in the middle of . . . what? I couldn't imagine what an invasion would be like, but I squeezed my eyes tight for a moment and thought the safest thoughts I could towards him. Not praying, exactly, just hoping he knew I was thinking good thoughts for him.

The twins were so excited, almost gloating, as though they'd planned the whole thing themselves, but then they didn't have anyone who was likely to be in danger. Their dad was a mechanic at an RAF air base, looking after the planes and repairing them so they could fly again, just like my Uncle Arthur. It was really important work, but they weren't likely to be on their way over to Europe to fight.

~*~

The hall was still buzzing with chatter when Miss Young walked in and we all stood up. It took a good few moments for everyone to be quiet. Looking around the room at everyone's faces, I could see that some of the girls were looking as worried as I felt; they must have fathers, uncles or brothers in the forces and probably had no idea where they were right now.

"Good morning, girls," Miss Young started. "I'm sure that some of you will be aware that a new phase of the war has begun today. Our brave Allies are, as I speak, invading Europe with the intention of liberating those areas that have been under German control. . . ," she turned her head towards Monsieur Dupont and made the slightest bow, just a nod, really, ". . . just as the city of Rome was recently liberated.

"School will continue as usual, and I encourage you to be calm," she went on, "but as I know that you are all keen to hear how the situation develops, and many of us, myself included, have relatives who may be involved in this battle, we will gather here at one o'clock for a special assembly to listen to the news.

"Instead of the Lord's Prayer, we will end assembly today with a short time of silence, during which I want you all to think about and pray for all those in the armed forces. Then we will all sing 'Fight The Good Fight'."

We closed our eyes and bowed our heads.

~*~

Class One's morning lesson was supposed to be French with Monsieur Dupont, but by the time the twins had asked him how to say, "Take that, Hitler," and, "We will never surrender," in French, the whole class was in slightly hysterical giggles and he had lost control, so he quietened us down by telling us some of the things he had seen while travelling through occupied Europe to escape.

Some were good stories, of people helping each other regardless of which country they belonged to or which religion they followed, and others were not so good, of people being forced out of their homes because they followed a different religion or belonged to the "wrong" nationality.

By playtime, we were quiet and thoughtful, but the whole school was starting to feel more normal. The usual toys and games appeared in the playground, although I saw some girls with worried faces being hugged and comforted by friends.

All through the war, we had known that our relatives who were serving in the forces could be fighting anywhere at any time, but this was different. A big battle was going on and we could hear what had happened almost as soon as it happened just by switching on the radio. It felt strange to be carrying on with a normal day during all of that, but, just like the signs in the windows of bomb damaged shops, it was "business as usual."

~*~

Class One was on second sitting for lunch, and normally we would dawdle back, making it to our classroom by the skin of our teeth on the dot of one o'clock, but today we bolted down our lunch and hurried back from the church hall at the double, to make sure we didn't miss a minute of the news broadcast.

It felt odd to be having assembly in the afternoon, but the whole day was odd.

Miss Young had already switched on the wireless when we arrived, and it was warming up; the sound of the last few minutes of the previous broadcast getting louder. She twiddled the knob to tune out the crackly interference as much as possible and motioned for us all to sit quietly on the floor.

"Here is the news, read by Frederick Allen," the radio boomed.

"'D'" Day has come. Allied troops were landed under strong naval and air cover on the coast of Normandy early this morning.

"The Prime Minister has told the Commons that the Commanding Officers have reported everything going to plan so far, with beach landing still going on at midday, and mass airborne landings successfully made behind the enemy lines.

"More than four thousand ships, with several thousand smaller craft, have crossed the Channel; and some eleven thousand first-line aircraft can be drawn upon for the battle.

"His Majesty The King will broadcast at nine o'clock tonight."

The rest of the news was going to be reports from journalists who were watching the landings, so Miss Young switched off the set.

She looked at us all for a moment as though she didn't quite know what to say, but we solved that problem for her by cheering and clapping. It went on for so long that it seemed we couldn't stop. Even those of us who might have someone we loved involved in the attack felt so proud of all our Allied forces that we almost stopped worrying. We all felt that this was an important day.

~*~

At home, I didn't mention what had happened at all; I didn't think Audrey's school would have let the children listen to the news. Some of them were too little to understand and might have been scared, and Mummy and Daddy had been at work all day, so they probably wouldn't have heard. I'd forgotten that Mum and her friends at the nursery were allowed to have a radio on in the glass house.

"Have you heard the news, Tom?" she asked, glancing at Audrey and me as she spoke.

"Yes," replied Daddy, putting his cup down carefully on its saucer and looking seriously at her.

I spoke up, "I have, too. We had a special assembly today to listen to the one o'clock news, and we sang 'Fight The Good Fight' this morning.

On the news they said that the King is going to broadcast at nine o'clock tonight. Can I stay up to hear it?"

"Yes, Sylvie, provided you go straight to bed afterwards," Daddy agreed.

"What news? What's happened?" asked Audrey.

Mum and Daddy gave each other a "look" that somehow decided between them that Mummy would explain to Audrey.

Daddy started clearing the plates and filling the sink and I got down from the table to help him.

"All our soldiers and sailors and airmen, and all the men from America and all the other countries who have come over here to help, are going to France, Audrey," said Mummy carefully. "They're all working together to send the Germans back home so that all the countries they've taken over can be free again. The war could be over soon."

"Oh, good!" said Audrey. "Then we can have proper sweets!"

~*~

Audrey went to bed at her usual time. She would probably have fallen asleep during the King's broadcast anyway, and she didn't really understand what was going on. She thought being at war was normal because she was too little to remember how it was before the war.

I changed for bed so I could go straight up after the broadcast, and snuggled on the settee, squeezed in between Mum and Daddy.

"His Majesty The King," announced the news reader, and the King began to speak slowly and hesitantly, with that odd way he had of pronouncing the letter "r". He spoke very seriously and talked a lot about God, and how if it was God's will we would win the war. He asked for all his subjects, in Britain and across the world, to pray for the armed forces.

When he mentioned the Queen and said that she understood the "anxieties and cares of our womenfolk," I expected the usual little snort from Mum — she didn't think much of the Queen — but she was quiet, listening hard.

I was a bit bored with all the talk of God; I heard a lot about him, what with Brownies, Sunday School, and going to a church school. This was more like a church service than a speech, but one sentence the King said really stuck in my mind:

"At this historic moment, surely not one of us is too busy, too young, or too old to play a part in a nationwide, a worldwide vigil of prayer as the great Crusade sets forth."

I didn't know about a Crusade, but the way he said it made me feel that even a child like me, even someone as young as Audrey, was part of this whole war. We were all going without things, either because of rationing, or because the things were needed elsewhere; Mum had given up some of her saucepans so the government could have enough metal to make planes; so we were all fighting in our own way.

The King finished his speech and Daddy turned the wireless off. "Off to bed with you, young lady," he said, pulling me up off the settee and giving me a hug. "School tomorrow."

I hugged him back, and climbed back onto the settee on my knees to hug Mum.

I knew we were all thinking about Uncle Johnny, but I didn't want to mention his name. If we didn't talk about him being in danger, it somehow kept him safe.

"Goodnight," said Mum. "Sleep tight, and mind the bugs don't bite." She smoothed my hair and kissed my cheek.

As I crept quietly up the stairs, avoiding that creaky board on the landing so as not to wake Audrey, I heard a whistled tune: "All The Nice Girls Love A Sailor," and I grinned to myself, thinking what Grandma would say if she heard Mum whistling.

"So unladylike, Amelia!"

Chapter Twenty-One

Campfire's Burning

The gathering outside the scout hut looked like a party of soldiers off to war, but in miniature. Eighteen girls in uniform, an assortment of adults, and a boy with a wooden barrow were milling around, waiting for the signal to march off.

Brown Owl was trying to do a head count, but every so often a wooly-hatted head bobbed up again in a different place and she lost count.

"Everyone please stand still for a moment!" she called, and we all froze, as if we were playing musical statues.

". . .seventeen, eighteen," counted Brown Owl. "Right, we're all here. Brownies, form up in your Sixes, two by two, and Tawny Owl bring up the rear, please. Mums, please follow along and pick up any stragglers."

Mr Perks, the greengrocer, helped his young assistant steady the wooden barrow, which was loaded with tents, bed rolls, cooking pots and utensils, bottles of lemonade, a bag of oats, and a small sack of potatoes, and waved us off.

We were going to Brownie camp!

We were only going as far as the grounds of Park Grange, just at the other end of the village, but it seemed like a big adventure, as most of us had never spent a night away from home before, and none of us had ever slept in a tent.

Mrs Fielding wasn't among the mums walking with us, and she had only allowed Maureen to come after Brown Owl herself had reassured her that we would be safe.

We all knew that if there was an air raid we were to go straight up to the house and down the kitchen stairs into the cellar. I knew the way, as I'd been in the house with Auntie Maude, so I promised Mrs Fielding that I'd take care of Maureen if we had to go to the shelter, even though she wasn't in my Six.

None of the mums were staying overnight; they were just coming to help us pitch camp and cook our tea. It would just be us Brownies, Brown Owl, and Tawny Owl.

~*~

The tents were a bit makeshift, but it was just for one night, and it was a hot August Saturday afternoon with no rain forecast.

Each six would be sharing a tent, and Brown Owl and Tawny Owl had another tent just for the two of them.

First, we had to ram the end poles into the ground to make an upside down V shape, and lash them together with rope so that they crossed at the top, making a smaller V for the ridge pole to sit in, then the long ridge pole was lashed in place.

A piece of tarpaulin was flung across the pole and pegged to the ground all round, with the ends tucked inside and one triangular end of the tent left open, then a groundsheet was laid on the floor inside the tent to cover the ends.

There was just room in each Brownie tent for six bed rolls to be laid out, end to end and side by side.

Some of us had proper bed rolls, a couple had sleeping bags borrowed from older brothers and sisters who were scouts or guides, but most of us had big blankets, folded into four, so that we could sleep on two layers with another two layers over the top of us.

The twins' mother asked where we were going to dig the latrine, but Brown Owl said that for one night's camping we could all use the servants' toilet off the kitchen passage. I didn't fancy going to the toilet in a hole in the ground anyway!

Brown Owl cleared a wide circle of ground free of grass and weeds, well away from the tents and the vegetable garden, and sent us all running into the copse beside the house to collect small dry sticks for kindling and bigger ones to build up the fire. By the time the last of us had run back and forth three times with wood, she had a good-sized camp fire burning merrily. She opened the sack of potatoes that Mr Perks had kindly given us and told one of the Sixers to fill a bucket with water from the outside tap in the kitchen garden, then we all chose our own potato from the sack and washed them in the bucket. By the time the last potato was washed we were putting more dirt back on them than we rubbed off, but this was camping. We were supposed to be roughing it a bit.

We had been saving up old pieces of tinfoil for weeks, and there was just enough to wrap all the potatoes, or at least keep them off the charred wood while they cooked.

While we waited for our tea to cook, Brown Owl sent us off on a tracking game.

That morning, she had gone all round the grounds of the house tying little pieces of coloured wool to plants, trees, garden ornaments, and door handles. Now, she gave each Sixer a short piece of wool: yellow for the Imps, Maureen's Six, green for the Sprites, and blue for my Six, the Pixies. We had an hour to search anywhere in the grounds to find twenty pieces of wool that matched the one we'd been given and bring them back to camp. The Six who found all their pieces of wool first would win the camp trophy, a small silver cup that was sitting in Brown Owl's tent.

"On your marks, get set, go!" Brown Owl blew her whistle and we scattered in our Sixes to all corners of the garden.

There was a lot of laughing as we bumped into other sixes looking in the same place for their pieces of wool, and it was fun to say, "Oh, I saw a yellow piece just over there," and point someone the wrong way, when actually their piece of wool was right behind them!

The Imps found all their pieces first and panted back to camp, shortly followed by us Pixies, but the Sprites were struggling; they had only one more piece to find and were running around more and more frantically, bumping into each other and treading on each other's feet. They still hadn't found the last piece of wool when Brown Owl blew her whistle for everyone to come back to camp, and their Sixer, Marion, looked miserable as they trooped sadly back with only nineteen pieces of wool.

~*~

Brown Owl had laid out our Magic Carpet, with flower pots placed on it for toadstools, and once we were all gathered back at camp we danced into our ring for the presentation of the camp trophy to the winning Six.

"You all did very well at the tracking game," said Brown Owl, "and it was very close between the Pixies and the Imps, but the Imps won, just seconds ahead of the Pixies. Tawny Owl, please bring the trophy over, and Imps, step forward to collect your prize."

The Imps proudly lined up in front of Brown Owl, but as Tawny Owl handed the cup to her older sister we all burst out laughing. There was the last piece of green wool, tied to one of the handles of the cup!

Even the Sprites laughed; Brown Owl had managed to fool everyone, but she had said *anywhere* in the grounds!

~*~

The potatoes were ready, and the mums, armed with oven gloves and sticks, pulled them out of the fire. Each potato was split in two and a little marge and salt put on them. There were a few burnt tongues as people tried to eat them straight away without letting them cool, and I made sure that I sat near Maureen while we ate, as I knew she wouldn't eat the skin of her potato if it was blackened, and that was the best part!

Bottles of lemonade were passed around, while Brown Owl filled a billycan with water and Tawny Owl rigged up a gadget from sticks to hang the can over the fire to boil water for tea for the mums.

While the grown-ups drank their tea, we washed our plates and forks in a bucket of water and then we were given another game to play. We had all been told to save any empty matchboxes in the few weeks before camp, and now we were given one each and told to go off again around the grounds and fill the matchboxes with as many tiny things as possible. The Brownie who collected the most different things in her box would win a much-coveted bar of chocolate!

We scattered around the gardens again, but this time it was every Brownie for herself. Some headed for the ornamental gardens to fill their boxes with pieces of different coloured gravel, others picked as many different leaves as they could find, but I had a bright idea. I waited until no-one was looking, then slipped around the back of the kitchen to the yard by the garage where the pigeon loft was. I knew from Auntie Maude that the pigeons were fed around tea time, and sure enough, there was a lot of spilled seed on the ground beside the loft. Pigeons are messy eaters!

I crouched down and sorted through the seeds. There were at least ten different types of seeds there, and that would give me a really good head start, as they were so tiny.

I picked up as many different seeds as I could find, then ran round to the flower garden. Lots of plants had finished flowering now, and when the Whitefields still had lots of gardeners at Park Grange, they would have been cut back and tidied up, but there was no-one to do that now, so all the flowers had gone to seed. I moved carefully from one plant to the next, taking one seed from each dried-up flower head and slipping it into my matchbox.

Brown Owl's whistle blew just as I was tapping a tiny poppy seed into my box from its pepper pot seed head, and I joined the rest of the pack running back to camp.

Each Brownie emptied her matchbox carefully onto a tea plate, and Brown Owl, Tawny Owl and the mums counted all the tiny things, writing the total on a slip of paper with each Brownie's name beside it. The slips were handed to Brown Owl and she sat on the floor of her tent to read through them all while we stood in a ring around Tawny Owl and played a game of catch. She threw a tennis ball high in the air, called out the name of a Brownie, then dodged back into the circle as the person whose name was called ran into the middle to catch the ball. They then threw the ball up and called out another name. We were all breathless and laughing by the time Brown Owl came back. Tawny Owl was in the centre of the circle, about to throw the ball again, and she smiled wickedly when she saw her sister walking towards her with her hand full of paper slips. "Brown Owl!" she called, throwing the ball as high as she could, and Brown Owl ran laughing into the circle, catching the ball one handed as she held the paper slips safely in the other hand.

"Gather round, Brownies," she said, tossing the ball back to her sister with a grin. She shuffled through the slips of paper in her hands, reading the numbers again.

"You have been so clever with this game!" she exclaimed. "I had no idea that there were so many tiny things in this garden! The winner of the matchbox game is. . . . Sylvie Ford, who managed to collect thirty-two different seeds! Well done, Sylvie!"

I stepped forward and returned Brown Owl's salute as she handed me my prize — the most enormous bar of chocolate I had seen since the war started!

"There's enough here for everyone to have a piece!" I said, holding the bar above my head for everyone to see. "Let's share it!"

The sun was starting to dip lower now, and the mums gathered up their things to leave camp. A couple of the youngest Brownies were a bit tearful, and I felt a few butterflies in my tummy seeing Mum getting ready to leave, but she gave me a brisk kiss on the top of my Brownie hat and said, "See you tomorrow, Chicken. Well done on winning that game, and good girl for sharing."

We waved the mums off until they were out of sight, then Brown Owl blew her whistle and we all stood to attention.

"Everyone make a ring around the camp fire," she said. "Sit together in your Sixes and we'll share out that bar of chocolate, eh, Sylvie?" She smiled at me and I handed her the chocolate to break up into twenty pieces.

We washed the chocolate down with the last of the lemonade, then Tawny Owl ran up to the house and came back with a guitar and a tambourine. She handed the tambourine to her sister and plucked at the strings of the guitar, adjusting the knobs at the end of the neck to make it sound right.

We started with the Brownie Song, la-la-ing it first and then singing the words, as we always did at our meeting, and as the last notes of the tune died away, Brown Owl tapped her tambourine and started on "Ten Green Bottles".

The sun was going down behind the house as we finished off the last green bottle and the fire was starting to die. Brown Owl prodded the embers and the flames danced higher.

"Does everyone know 'Camp Fire's Burning'?" she asked. Some Brownies shook their heads, so she nodded to Tawny Owl to start playing and they sang the words slowly so that everyone could learn it. The tune was the same as "London's Burning".

Campfire's burning, campfire's burning,
Draw nearer, draw nearer,
In the gloaming, in the gloaming,
Come sing and be merry.

We sang it together twice, until everyone knew it by heart, then Tawny Owl played a chord on her guitar and announced, "Now we're going to sing it in a round. Pixies, you start, then when they've finished the first line, Imps start, from "campfire's burning", then Sprites, when the Imps finish the first line you start, and Brown Owl and I will come in last. When you finish the song, start all over again!"

She strummed the guitar and hummed the tune for us to start, and nodded for each Six to start their round. The first attempt was a bit of a muddle, but eventually we all got the hang of it, and it sounded wonderful, all the different parts of the tune overlapping and weaving around each other, not a sound in the garden except the guitar, our voices, and the birds, singing their own evening songs.

Tawny Owl gently signaled for each Six to stop singing as they ended their verse, and she and Brown Owl were left finishing their last "Come sing and be merry" alone.

Brown Owl stood up. "Brownies, please stand for Taps."

We stood to attention and Tawny Owl plucked the first note on her guitar so we could sing together:

"Day is done,
Gone the sun,
From the sea,
From the hills,
From the sky,
All is well,
Safely rest,
God is nigh."

We saluted, and each Six mimed throwing "fairy dust" into the fire as they marched away to their tent. Brown Owl and Tawny Owl threw theirs last and stayed to bank the fire while we all crawled into our bed rolls.

I could hear someone sniffing and whimpering from one of the Brownie tents, and giggling from the other, but ours was quiet. From my bedroll by the tent opening, I could see the sky getting darker, and watched as the first few stars popped out. I sighed happily and folded my hands behind my head, thinking about all the animals scurrying about in the copse, some going to bed and some getting up to go out hunting for food.

Brown Owl and Tawny Owl muttered soft goodnights to everyone, and I heard rustling from their tent as they settled down.

The stars were getting brighter now and I started to count them.

One, two three. . . .

~*~

I woke the next morning to the clatter of plates and crawled out of the tent. A few Brownies were already up and helping Brown Owl re-lay the fire and set out plates for breakfast, but the whistle hadn't been blown for everyone to get up yet.

Tawny Owl came across the damp grass from the kitchen with a bucket of cold water and poured it into a big metal pot with handfuls of oats and a little salt. Porridge for breakfast!

Brown Owl smiled as she saw me emerge from my tent.

"Good morning, Sylvie. Run up to the kitchen garden and join the queue for a wash. I'll be blowing the whistle for everyone to get up soon, and you can all help stir the porridge so that it doesn't stick."

There was a lot of chatter as we lined up to take our turn at the outside tap. Someone had heard an owl in the night, and there had been great excitement in the Imps' tent when a fox had put its head through the opening, but I had slept soundly through all of it. I shook the water drops off my hands, watching them make rainbows in the morning sun, and ran back to camp as the whistle blew.

The last sleepy-heads crawled out of their tents and stumbled off to wash the sleep out of their eyes while the rest of us took turns at stirring the porridge. Maureen grumbled and complained that she wasn't going to eat any, she hated porridge, but it didn't matter, as we were going home after breakfast, once we'd struck camp. The Brownies had been excused church parade today because of the camp, but Brown Owl and Tawny Owl had to go with their Guide Company, so we needed to be back at the scout hut by nine to give them time to change.

~*~

We were just washing the last of the dishes when Mr Perks' boy came rumbling his cart down the garden path and rested it against a tree while he helped Brown Owl and Tawny Owl to take down the tents and fold everything. Taking the camp apart was much quicker than putting it up!

As we marched down the drive to the road, I looked back at the quiet garden, the dew rising from the grass as mist. It was a garden again now and not a camp site. I'd had such a good time, and couldn't wait to tell everyone at home about it. I did hope Mum hadn't already told them about me winning the matchbox game.

Brown Owl took one final head count as we milled around once again at the scout hut, then dismissed us with a wave and a smile. Maureen and I ran all the way home, and said a quick goodbye at our front doors.

The rest of my family were just finishing breakfast as I ran into the front room, and I burst into the kitchen, ready to tell them all about camp, but Audrey got in first.

"Guess what, Sylvie?" she cried.

I couldn't guess, but it had to be something jolly good as they were all smiling broadly.

"The war's over?" I asked.

"Not quite that good, but almost," said Mum, handing me a postcard.

I read the words aloud;

"Back in Blighty safe and sound. If that was a beach holiday, I don't think much of it. Home as soon as I can get leave.

Johnny."

Part Seven
1945

Chapter Twenty-Two

A Bad Sunday

"I'm bored with going to church," said Maureen as we trudged along, heads down against the cold wind. "Let's not go this week."

I could see her point. We had spent rather a lot of time in church over Christmas, what with parades with the Brownies, the carol service with school, not to mention ordinary church and Sunday school.

"But what shall we do instead?" I asked. "Where can we go? We can't just go home, or they'll know we've bunked off, and it's too cold to just hang around outside."

Maureen trudged on, thinking.

"I know, let's go up the allotments. I've got a key to the shed."

It didn't seem like much of a fun way to spend a Sunday morning, but I completely agreed with her about being fed up with church, and now we were ten, Sunday school seemed a bit babyish. We could be back in time for the late morning service at eleven that we usually went to with our parents, and no-one would be any the wiser.

"Come on, then," I said, "quick, before anyone sees us, or we'll have to go."

We slipped through the gate at the side of the churchyard and up the lane past the cemetery, turning left down the track to the allotments. There wouldn't be anyone working up there on a Sunday morning in January. Even the most devoted vegetable growers wouldn't try to break up the frozen soil today.

Maureen unlocked the shed door and we stamped our feet and blew out steaming breath as we tried to get a bit warmer. There was no heating in the shed, so it wasn't that much warmer than being outside, but at least it was sheltered from the cold wind.

Maureen turned a bucket upside down and pushed it across the floor with her foot for me to sit on, and unfolded an old deckchair that had half the canvas of the back hanging off.

We sat in silence for a while. Surely bunking off should be more fun than this? I was starting to think I'd rather be in Sunday school.

"So are you going to sit the scholarship exam after Easter?" asked Maureen.

"Yes, I suppose so," I replied, fiddling with the cuffs of my woolly gloves. "Mum and Dad haven't said I'm not to."

Maureen nodded glumly. She wouldn't be sitting the exam, as she was going to leave school at fourteen and start work. It was what she wanted to do, but I knew why she was sad. If I passed the scholarship exam, I would still have another year to do at the Big Girls', but in the third year the class was split in two; Class Three A would do lessons more similar to the kind of thing we'd be expected to do at the Grammar School, but Class Three B, those staying on to fourteen, would carry on with the same sort of lessons we'd always done, just a bit harder.

If I passed the exam, we wouldn't be in the same class any more, and we'd shared a desk at school ever since we were four coming five in Miss Eames' class.

"We can still walk to school and home together," I encouraged her, "and there'll be playtimes and lunchtime, and it's not as if we live miles apart, is it!"

"I suppose not", Maureen grudgingly admitted, "but it won't be the same."

"Why don't you try for the scholarship?" I asked her.

"I'm not clever like you," she said. "You know I hate maths, and I'm always asking you for spellings. Besides, Mum will need me to start work as soon as I can leave school, as we don't know where Dad is or if. . . ."

She didn't finish the sentence and I knew what she didn't want to say. Mrs Fielding had received a telegram just before Christmas saying that her husband was "missing believed captured".

He had been posted to Italy and was believed to be in a prisoner of war camp somewhere.

We had tried to keep Maureen and her mum cheerful, inviting them to Grandma's with us for Christmas Dinner, and spending as much time with them as possible to take their minds off it, but I knew how they felt; it had been horrible all the time when we didn't know where Uncle Johnny was.

"Let's talk about something more cheerful," I said. "That new Googie Withers film is on at the Empire next week. Shall we go?"

"What do you reckon her real name is?" asked Maureen. "No-one's christened Googie, surely?"

"Maybe it's short for Gooseberry," I suggested and Maureen snorted with laughter.

"Or maybe it's. . . ." she stopped suddenly.

"What?"

"Shh . . . listen. I thought I heard. . . ."

A huge bang shook the air itself. It seemed too loud to even be real, and the whole sky lit up in a flash of white light that only lasted an instant, so short that we weren't even sure afterwards that we'd really seen it. We dived under the potting bench in the shed and hung onto each other for dear life. Pots were falling from the shelves, something big crashed down at the other end of the shed, and the ground shook. Then there was silence.

We sat up and looked at each other.

"I didn't hear a siren, did you?" Maureen whispered.

"No," I replied. "Nothing, just bang. It sounded really close."

We helped each other to our feet and started moving all the fallen pots and boxes to get to the door.

All we could smell when we opened the door was smoke. A big plume of black smoke was billowing up into the sky from just beyond the church tower. I wondered if I looked as pale as Maureen.

"Come on, run!" I shouted. "We need to get home — there might be another one."

"No!" screamed Maureen. "We should get to a shelter!"

"I'm going home." I yelled in her face. "Are you coming or not?"

We held hands and ran as fast as we could, not back the way we'd come, that was towards the smoke, but out the other end of the allotments onto the road and back around to the main street.

People were running in all directions, some, carrying buckets and fire hoses, towards the explosion and others, in their smart Sunday clothes, coming the other way, the early church service having been abruptly ended.

As we passed the church, we saw that the big stained glass windows on the two sides closest to the explosion had been completely blown out. Some of the people coming out of the church were holding handkerchiefs to cuts and grazes where pieces of flying glass had hit them.

We could see now that the plume of smoke was up the hill, behind the cemetery, and well away from our houses, but we still ran as though something terrifying was following us.

Maureen's front door was standing wide open, and Daddy was in our own front door, pulling on his Fire Watcher's helmet and trying to calm a hysterical Mrs Fielding, who was sobbing in Mum's arms. Audrey was standing behind them, her face as white as a sheet and tears running down her face.

"Mummy!" yelled Maureen, and ran up the path.

Daddy turned and glared at us. I had never seen that look on his face before and I never wanted to see it again.

"Where the *hell* have you two been?" he shouted.

I stopped still, my eyes filling with tears. I had never heard Daddy swear before.

"Never mind, Tom," said Mum. "They're safe, that's all that matters. I'll deal with this, you go and help. And if you see Micky, tell him the girls are safe; he'll be wanted up there, too."

Daddy grabbed me in a quick hug and kissed the top of my head so hard I could feel his teeth behind his lips. I realised that he had been angry because he was worried and frightened. I had never seen an adult that frightened before.

Mum pulled us into the house and helped us out of our coats, trying to quieten Mrs Fielding and comfort Audrey at the same time. She pushed us quite roughly onto the settee and stood over us, arms folded.

"Now then, you two, listen to me. I don't know where you've been and I don't care, but let me just tell you this. When that explosion went off and your Dad went out looking for you, Sylvie, and everyone he met coming from the church said they hadn't seen you, how do you think we felt? You could have been anywhere. You could have been. . . ."

She choked off the last words and her eyes filled with tears.

I jumped up and flung myself into her arms, sobbing, and she held me tight, stroking my hair and murmuring, "There, there, it's all right, we're all safe," over and over.

Maureen was clinging to her mum, and Audrey was kneeling in the middle of the floor, her face buried in Scamp's fur as she sobbed.

"If ye're all safe what's all the keenin' about?" came a voice from the door, and we all turned tear-streaked faces to Micky.

His eyebrow was quirked in that way he had, and he looked so comical that we couldn't help laughing.

"Everyone here is safe, Micky, thank you," said Mum, blowing her nose. "Tom's gone up there to see if he can help. Do you know what happened? Is anyone. . . ?"

"It was one of those rocket things, what do they call them? V2. They just come out of nowhere with no warning, they're so fast. They don't think anyone was hurt bad; it landed in the empty field behind the cemetery. So far, everyone's accounted for, but there's a lot of damage. The cemetery chapel is near destroyed, and there'll be a big job for the glass companies, fixing all those windows up there, so there will. I'd better be getting back up there. I just saw someone who said he'd seen Tom go out with a face like thunder, and I wanted to make sure you were all safe."

He tipped his hat and limped off up the road.

We all flopped down onto the nearest seat, wiping our eyes, shaking with a mixture of fear and relief. Mum picked Audrey up and sat her on her lap, big girl of six though she was, and soothed her until she stopped crying.

Mrs Fielding stood up. "I don't know about all of you, but I need a cup of tea," she said.

"Come on, Maureen, make yourself useful and help me."

I looked at Mummy and reached out to hold her hand.

"I'm sorry, Mummy," I said, tears welling up again.

She squeezed my hand. "Just so long as you're alright, my chick. Now, let's all have a cuppa, then you and Maureen keep an eye on Audrey while Mrs Fielding and I go and see if there's anything we can do to help."

~*~

It was a long day. We played snakes and ladders for what seemed like hours, and it was still only mid-day. The adults still hadn't come back by one o'clock, so Maureen and I made sandwiches with whatever we could find in the larder for ourselves and Audrey.

It was getting dark and we were just on our third game of Ludo when the door opened and Mummy and Daddy walked in, with Mrs Fielding, Micky, and Auntie Helen.

"That's good girls," said Daddy. He sat down wearily in

the armchair and started to change his work boots for his best shoes.

"No-one's hurt, apart from a few broken bones and some cuts and scrapes. We met the vicar on the way back, and he's going to open the church up for evening service as usual. The verger and the warden have been sweeping up all afternoon and there's no structural damage to the church. Do you girls want to come? I think we've got quite a lot to be thankful for today."

I looked at Maureen and she stared back at me. The morning seemed like years ago. I thought she was never going to say anything, so I took her coat down from the hook and held it out for her to put her arms in.

"Come on," I said. "We're going to church."

Chapter Twenty-Three

Testing Times

Mum slipped a coin into my hand as she left for work, "Here's two shillings," she said, kissing my cheek. "Treat yourself to lunch at the café on the green. It's not worth you walking all the way home to an empty house and having to go all the way back again."

"Thank you, Mummy!" I hugged her and waved her off down the path.

I didn't need to leave for another hour at least; the morning exam was at ten o'clock. I wandered aimlessly around the house, Scamp trotting behind me wondering why I was still at home.

My stomach felt knotted with nerves. I looked at the clock again. Five minutes closer to time to leave.

I checked my satchel one more time. Writing pencils, my scratchy school pen, ruler, protractor, set square, coloured pencils, rubber, and something else? I rummaged at the bottom of the bag and pulled out a tiny Kewpie doll with a sign hanging round its neck that read in wonky letters "gOOd Luk SyLvie". Audrey.

I smiled and tucked the doll back into the bottom of the satchel, fastening the buckle again.

It was no good; I couldn't settle to anything, so I decided to set out early and go for a walk in the park; maybe some fresh air would calm my nerves.

Daddy had wished me luck when he left for work and told me to stop worrying. "You can only do your best, Sylvie, and if you can honestly say you've done that, then Mummy and I will be happy, whatever the result."

I knew he was right, and I knew I could re-take the exam if I failed, provided there were still places available at the Grammar school, but at the moment it seemed that passing this exam was the most important thing that would ever happen in my life.

There was someone sitting on my favourite bench in the park, the one that overlooked the duck pond. I perched on the other end of the bench and glanced sideways. It was Jasmine from my class!

We smiled at each other shyly; I didn't know her very well, she was a very sporty girl and spent most of her break times with other girls who were in the netball team or the rounders team, while the most athletic thing Maureen and I did was playing ball-up-the-wall.

"Are you going for the scholarship exam?" she asked.

I nodded. "You too?"

"Yes," she said. "I was so so nervous, I couldn't sit still at home, so I came out for a walk, but I'm still nervous," she admitted.

"Me too." I grinned. "At least we can be nervous together!"

"Do you think it'll be very hard?" she asked, chewing at the skin around her thumbnail.

"I don't know," I replied, swinging my feet to shoo away a pigeon that thought we might have food. "They can't make it too hard, or no-one would ever get in."

"They won't expect us to know Latin, will they?" she asked, wide eyed.

I hadn't thought of that.

We trailed slowly down the hill to the Grammar School. We were still ten minutes early, but we decided it was better to turn up early and look keen than be late.

We weren't the only ones who were early. There was a small knot of children gathered in front of the main door of the school, a few with their mothers.

Some of the children were in uniforms, boys in grey shorts and blazers, with caps and ties, and girls in pinafores and straw boaters. Children from schools all over the district entered the scholarship exam, and some of these children looked as though they went to very posh schools.

I had put on an outfit that I thought looked the most like a school uniform that I could manage: a grey flannel skirt, a white blouse, and a lemon cardigan. Maybe the pink kitten sewn onto the front of the cardigan didn't look quite right.

The big double doors opened slowly and everyone fell silent.

"Good morning, everyone," said a tall, thin elderly man.

"Good morning, Sir," we all replied, the mothers too.

The man introduced himself as Mr Howard, the headmaster, and invited us into the building.

We all tiptoed in quietly. The school was so quiet, no-one wanted to speak or shuffle their feet.

"The examination will take place in the hall," said Mr Howard, pointing to a pair of double doors with glass panels at the top.

"Mr Allen, the head of Mathematics, will invigilate."

Good for him, I thought, looking round to see if anyone else knew what he was talking about. Some of them nodded wisely, but I bet they didn't know, either.

A short, bustling man with very thick, small round glasses perched on the end of his nose hurried towards us and the headmaster introduced him as Mr Allen.

"Thank you, headmaster," he said, in a surprisingly high voice. "Students, from the moment you enter the hall you are to remain in complete silence. There is to be no talking during the exam, and if you need to leave the room you must raise a hand and wait to be spoken to, understand?"

"Yes, Sir," we murmured.

"Please file in and each of you stand behind a desk. You may choose any desk."

We silently marched into the hall. It was a huge room, much bigger than the hall at my school, and panelled with wood on every wall. There were pictures of kings and queens hanging around the room, with a painting of the current King and Queen above a small stage at the front, where a teacher's desk and chair were placed. I assumed that was where Mr Allen would be doing that invigi . . . thing from.

Single desks and chairs were dotted around the room, an exam paper face down on each, with plenty of space between the desks so no-one could possibly see what anyone else was writing, or copy anyone's work.

I stood behind a desk near the wall, feeling somehow safer there than being in the middle of the room.

Mr Allen climbed onto the stage and stood watching over his glasses until all of us were standing to attention in our places.

"You may sit and get out your writing things," he said, "but do not touch the paper until I tell you to."

We sat down with a scrape of chairs and arranged our pencil cases on the desks.

"Please turn over the paper and write your name in block capitals at the top," we were instructed.

Mr Allen turned to look at the clock behind him. The second hand was ticking towards 10 o'clock.

"You may begin," he announced. "Answer all the questions, and show your workings."

The only sounds in the room were the ticking of the clock, the scratching of pencils, and the occasional cough or sigh.

Working out a calculation in my head, I looked up and gazed blankly forward. Mr Allen caught my glance and glared. I felt myself go red and looked back down at my paper.

The sums at the start were quite easy, even the long division, but the later questions got harder. Questions about angles in a triangle, measuring the height of a tree, and one very complicated question about how long it would take three men with three buckets to empty a bath if it took one man with one bucket an hour. Why didn't they just pull the plug out? I thought, but I ploughed through the question and showed my workings.

~*~

"Five minutes left."

The voice from the front of the hall made me jump. I had been so engrossed in the paper that I'd forgotten where I was.

I finished the last answer and quickly checked through the paper. I had written as clearly and neatly as possible, and answered all the questions. That was the best I could do.

"Pencils down, hands in laps," the stern teacher said.

He walked briskly up and down the rows collecting the papers then returned to his desk and shuffled them fussily until they were in a neat pile.

"You may leave. No talking until you are outside the examination room."

~*~

Jasmine left the hall ahead of me and turned and waited. She puffed out her cheeks and crossed her eyes. "Whew! That was awful! What a strict man!" she whispered. "I hope all the teachers aren't like that!"

I agreed with her. If they were all as stern as him I wasn't too sure I wanted to come to this school.

"Do you think you did all right?" asked Jasmine.

"I don't know," I said worriedly. "I answered all the questions. I'm not sure whether I got them all right."

"Oh, well, you did better than me then. I ran out of time and didn't finish the last two, and the one about the bath . . . why didn't they just pull the plug out?"

We laughed and ran down the steps and out of the gates.

"Are you going home for lunch?" I asked her. "I've got two shillings to buy something to eat at the café. We can share if you like."

Jasmine rummaged in her skirt pocket. "I've got one and six," she said, producing the coins. "We can have a real slap up lunch for that!"

Andrea Gilbey

~*~

Full of tea and egg sandwiches, we made our way back to the school for the afternoon exam. Some of the other children were standing around outside the front door, not knowing whether they were supposed to wait, knock, or just walk in.

As we discussed what to do, the door opened, and a small, smiling lady with red-gold hair cut in a smooth bob appeared.

"Ah, there you are! In you come, children. Is everyone here?"

We looked around and one of the boys in uniform said "Two more to come, Miss. Here they come, now."

"Good, you're all very punctual, well done!" She smiled.

When we were all gathered in the lobby outside the hall, she smiled again, looking at all of us individually.

"My name is Mrs Fleming, and I'm the head of English," she said. "Please go in and find a desk. I will tell you what to do next."

Jasmine and I grinned at each other as we walked into the hall. What a nice lady! Maybe not all the teachers were strict here.

We stood behind our desks as we had in the morning. The hall felt quite familiar now and not as frightening as it had earlier.

"Please sit down," said Mrs Fleming. "This afternoon's paper has three parts. The first part is a comprehension test. You will read a passage taken from a book called Silas Marner, by George Eliot, and there are six questions to answer about what you have read. You must answer in full sentences, paying attention to spelling and grammar, and of course in your very best writing." She smiled again. "The second part," she continued, "consists of a passage of text which I want you to punctuate as best you can. The third part is creative writing." I grinned broadly as she said that, and she caught my eye and almost winked.

"I want you all to write an essay on the subject of 'Friendship'".

One of the uniformed boys put up his hand and Mrs Fleming nodded to him. "Yes?"

"Please, Miss." He spoke nervously. "We've never written essays before."

Mrs Fleming looked around the room.

"Has anyone here ever written an essay?"

We all shook our heads.

"Who here has studied French?" she asked and several of us put up our hands.

"Who can tell me the meaning of the verb 'essayer'?"

I put my hand up again, and she nodded for me to speak.

"It means 'to try', Miss," I replied.

"Good girl." I beamed at her praise. "So, the word essay simply means to try. That's all you need to do, try. Write what you know about friendship. Keep in mind your grammar and spelling, but enjoy yourselves and express yourselves. Ready? Then turn over your papers and begin."

As we worked, Mrs Fleming strolled between the desks, nodding encouragement and smiling at any of us who looked up.

I finished the comprehension test quickly, and concentrated hard on the punctuation test. It was much easier without Maureen huffing and puffing beside me.

I started a fresh, clean piece of paper for the essay and wrote the title "Friendship" neatly at the top in the centre.

I sat quietly for a minute thinking hard. Thinking about all the friends I had, my school friends, Ruby the Land Girl, Micky, Auntie Helen, who had changed from a teacher to a friend, and my family. Audrey was old enough now to be a friend as well as a sister, and as I grew older Mum and Daddy were staring to treat me more like a friend as well as a daughter.

What made a friend?

I took up my pencil and started to write.

Chapter Twenty-Four

Victory!

"Have a good day, girls, and be good." Daddy leaned across his bike and kissed Mum on the cheek. "You too," he winked at her.

Audrey and I hitched up our satchels and turned to say goodbye, but stopped in surprise, seeing Mrs Fielding, curlers still in, batting on the broken top pane of glass in the lean-to door. It had cracked when the rocket fell and no-one had any glass to spare to mend it, so it was held together with brown tape.

Daddy opened the door and Mrs Fielding almost fell in, red in the face and out of breath. Maureen came running in behind her.

"Elsie! Whatever's the matter?"

I had never heard Mum or Mrs Fielding call each other by their first names before.

"Hitler's dead!" panted Mrs Fielding.

"Oh no, the poor chicken!" Audrey piped up. We all gave her a look.

"Not the cockerel, dear, that silly man with the ridiculous moustache who caused all this war. He shot himself yesterday. Best day's work he ever did, if you ask me." Mrs Fielding folded her arms, defying anyone to argue with her, but we weren't going to; we all just stood there with gaping mouths.

"Where did you hear that?" asked Mum.

"On the wireless just now. It was on the BBC news, so it must be true. And they said it twice. If it was April the first I might have doubted it, but it's May the first."

"Does that mean the war's over?" I asked.

"Not yet," said Daddy, "but it can't last much longer now. The German high command has been a shambles for a long while, and now Hitler's gone they'll fight among themselves. They may as well surrender now."

We all looked at each other in silent amazement, then Mum broke the spell.

"Look at the time, you'll be late, girls, off you go."

~*~

The school playground was buzzing with excitement, and it seemed that the staff room must have been talking about the news, too, as the bell for lessons was ten minutes late.

The atmosphere all day was like the week before Christmas. Everyone was too excited to concentrate properly, even the teachers.

On the way home from school we saw groups of people standing around talking excitedly. The war would soon be over!

None of the news reports said it in so many words, but everyone knew that it was just a matter of days before an official announcement was made.

~*~

Finally, on May the seventh, official hints started to appear, although still no announcement had been made.

Red white and blue cotton material came off ration for the rest of the month, provided it cost no more than one and three for a square yard, and bunting, rosettes and flags appeared in shop window displays, the front windows of houses, and strung across streets. Mum made us each a little rosette to pin to our coat lapels, and Audrey insisted on wearing red white and blue ribbons in her hair, which made doing her plaits each morning take twice as long.

It was announced that bonfires would be allowed, so long as nothing was burned that could have been salvaged and used. Boys with trolleys, wheelbarrows and carts charged around the streets after school collecting up any scrap wood they could find, and a huge bonfire started to take shape on the edge of the damaged wasteland where the rocket had fallen.

Bell ringers were told to get ready to ring a peal in celebration, but still no announcement came.

It was like Christmas morning when you get up and see all your presents under the tree, but can't touch them yet! The whole country was holding its breath, waiting for the signal to celebrate.

If you were out in the street when the news came on the wireless, you would have thought the village was deserted; everyone was gathered around their set or a neighbour's set, waiting.

Finally, it was official. At twenty to eight that evening the announcement came, just in time for Audrey, as she went to bed at eight.

"In accordance with arrangements between the three great powers, tomorrow, Tuesday, will be treated as Victory in Europe Day and will be regarded as a holiday."

Wednesday was also to be a holiday. Two days off school!

~*~

This was going to be the biggest party ever, and only one day to get ready! Neighbours ran back and forth all evening, sharing rations, borrowing serving dishes, baking tins, cooking pots, combining whatever they could find in their larder cupboards to get together a big feast for the whole street.

Lights burned in kitchen windows until late into the night, and clattering could be heard in every attic and cupboard as people pulled out flags and decorations.

The sun was barely up when the street burst into life. Any table that could be moved was called into service. Pasting tables, card tables and garden tables were lined up in a row of uneven heights along the middle of the street and covered with assorted linen tablecloths. Every chair in every house was dragged outside; no-one had time to sit down anyway.

Children ran errands, begged cutlery, plates and cups, and generally got in the way, laughing and screaming with excitement, and for once no-one was threatened with tears before bedtime.

Audrey and I collided with the post lady on our front path as we dashed out carrying cushions to put on the highest chairs for the smallest children to sit on, and she laughed and slid the post onto the hall table.

By mid-afternoon, everything was ready. A sudden quiet fell, like the hush that comes before family arrive for a big party, when the last preparations are finished and there's nothing to do but sit and wait and avoid creasing your best dress.

Mr Churchill was due to broadcast to the nation at three o'clock and the street party would not start until the great man had spoken. We stood around the wireless, Maureen and Mrs Fielding making our solemn little group up to six, as the war in Europe officially ended.

"We may allow ourselves a brief period of rejoicing; but let us not forget for a moment the toil and efforts that lie ahead. Japan with all her treachery and greed, remains unsubdued.

"We must now devote all our strength and resources to the completion of our task, both at home and abroad. Advance Britannia."

It was over. Really over.

People trickled out into the streets, looking at each other in happy amazement. There was a jangling clatter from halfway down the road as someone dragged a piano into the street, and everyone laughed and started singing as Mrs Keele, an elegant, reserved lady who taught piano lessons in her spotless front room, sat down at the piano, grinned at her neighbours and rattled out "Roll Out The Barrel." She jangled on into "Roll me Over In The Clover"; we weren't supposed to know the words to that one, but we did. Further down the long table, I could see Maureen kicking up her legs in a can can and showing her drawers. Her mum would have her guts for garters if she saw that.

The food kept on coming, plate after plate after plate. Sandwiches, cakes, pies, puddings, some made from quite unusual ingredients, but no-one cared. Bottles of lemonade were passed down the table, and gallons of tea were brewed. Someone had fetched the giant tea urn from the church hall to keep the cups filled.

Running back into the house after one glass of lemonade too many, I collided with Mum who was coming the other way with a tray of biscuits.

"Oh, Sylvie." She steadied me and re-balanced her tray. "There's a letter for you on the hall table. I think it's from the Grammar School scholarship committee. You open it, and I'll deliver this and come straight back."

~*~

"Sylvie?"

I looked up, blank faced.

"Oh, darling, it doesn't matter, you can try again. . . ."

"No," I interrupted, "I did it. I got in, look."

I passed her the letter with a shaking hand.

"Oh! Where's Daddy?" She popped her head out the door and whistled. I wished I could whistle like that.

"Tom! Gather up Audrey and come here a minute."

They hurried in, Daddy looking worried. Audrey had a big slice of bread and jam in her hand and jam all round her face.

Mum handed the letter to Daddy. He read it quickly, then cleared his throat and read it again, out loud.

"The board and governors of Handley Grammar School are pleased to award a scholarship place to Sylvia Ford, and wish to commend her on attaining the highest marks in the district in the scholarship examination."

He cleared his throat again, and his eyes shone as he swooped me up into a hug.

"Well done, Ducks, I knew you could do it."

"Sylvie's going to the Grammar School!" yelled Audrey, and I hushed her quickly.

"I need to tell Maureen," I said, looking anxiously at Mum. "She should be the first to know after all of you. She's my best friend, but she'll be upset."

Mum hugged me. "Yes, she'll be upset, and you will miss being together all day, but she's a good friend and a generous girl and she'll be happy for you."

Just then Maureen herself ran in with her mum panting behind her.

"Sylvie! The post lady came this morning," she cried excitedly.

"Yes, I know, I just opened it and. . . ."

"Daddy's safe! He's coming home!" she held out a postcard that had been posted in Italy weeks ago, but had only just arrived.

"Am safe, home as soon as I can. Love, Gerald."

Mrs Fielding was crying and laughing at the same time, and after we had all cried and kissed and hugged them we shared my news.

Maureen squeezed me in a hug again.

"I told you you were clever!" she beamed.

"I think this calls for a special celebration," said Daddy, and disappeared into the kitchen, returning with three glasses and the rest of the bottle of whiskey that Micky had given him on a Christmas day that seemed a lifetime ago.

~*~

Maureen, Audrey, and I stood in doorway, holding hands in a circle of three. Audrey looked at us both in turn.

"What's it going to be like not to be in a war?" she asked.

I squeezed a hand of each of them.

"Let's go and find out!" And we ran out into the street to re-join the celebrations.

About the Author

Andrea Gilbey lives in leafy Hertfordshire with her two cats. She works full time in the fashion industry and enjoys drawing, painting, graphic art and photography to relax and unwind.

Andrea has published five illustrated children's books for pre-schoolers and upwards, and with Southern Indiana Writers colleague Ginny Fleming, worked on the Written in Our Hearts Cookbook in aid of the Davy Jones Equine Memorial Foundation.

Andrea's illustrations are inspired by friends, family and the world about her. She has written a non-fiction social history book, a children's novel, and is currently working on a sequel to Bottletops for Battleships.

Printed in Great Britain
by Amazon